SABOTAGE

SABOTAGE

Karen Autio

WINLAW, BRITISH COLUMBIA

LIBRARY AND ARCHIVES CANADA CATALOGUING IN PUBLICATION

Autio, Karen, 1958-, author
        Sabotage / Karen Autio.

ISBN 978-1-55039-208-1 (pbk.)

        1. Finnish Canadians—Ontario—Juvenile fiction. 2. World War,
1914-1918—Ontario—Juvenile fiction. 3. Ontario—Social conditions—
20th century—Juvenile fiction. I. Title.

PS8601.U85S38 2013   JC813'.6   C2013-901975-8

Sono Nis Press most gratefully acknowledges support for our
publishing program provided by the Government of Canada through
the Canada Book Fund and the Canada Council for the Arts, and by the
Province of British Columbia through the British Columbia Arts Council
and the Book Publishing Tax Credit, Ministry of Provincial Revenue.

This book is a work of fiction. Names, characters, places, and incidents are
either the product of the author's imagination or are used fictitiously.

Cover design by Frances Hunter and Jim Brennan
Interior design by Frances Hunter
Edited by Laura Peetoom
Copy edited by Dawn Loewen
Proofread by Audrey McClellan
Cover photo of girl by Doug Wilson
Cover photo of boy © Monika Adamczyk/Pavel Losevsky/Dreamstime.com
Cover photo of Canadian Pacific Railway Nipigon River bridge
    courtesy Nipigon Historical Museum Archives, NMP 1290
First verse of "Crossing the Water" used as the epigraph with the kind
    permission of Bill Staines

Published by   Distributed in the U.S. by
Sono Nis Press   Orca Book Publishers
Box 160   Box 468
Winlaw, BC V0G 2J0   Custer, WA 98240-0468
1-800-370-5228   1-800-210-5277

books@sononis.com
www.sononis.com

The Canada Council | Le Conseil des Arts
for the Arts | du Canada

Printed and bound in Canada by Houghton Boston Printers.
Printed on acid-free paper that is forest friendly (100% post-consumer
recycled paper) and has been processed chlorine free.

For all of the readers
who asked for more about John

S. D. G.

AUTHOR'S NOTE

This is a work of historical fiction. While some events in this book are historically accurate (e.g., the sinking of the Canadian Pacific steamship *Empress of Ireland* on May 29, 1914), others were moved forward in time to aid the flow of the story (e.g., the attack on the Port Arthur government wireless telegraph station). The International Co-Operative Trading Company, which operated the Co-Op grocery store, went bankrupt in the spring of 1915. For the purposes of this book, the store continues to operate later into that year.

All women (and their children) who were interned with their German husbands during the First World War were sent to the Vernon Internment Camp. As it happened, all of these women and children were from Vancouver and Victoria, British Columbia. However, if a woman from elsewhere in Canada had chosen to be interned along with her German husband, she and any children would have been sent to Vernon. Letters written by internees were censored, with any details about internment operations blackened. For the sake of the story, I allowed Birgitta liberties in writing about life in the Vernon Internment Camp.

The *Port Arthur Daily News* (renamed the *Daily News-Chronicle* in February 1916) provided a wealth of information about events and opinion from 1914 through 1916. To see interesting items from Port Arthur newspapers, please visit my website at www.karenautio.com.

The characters in this book are fictional except for the following, in order of reference or appearance: John James (J. J.) Carrick, Member of Parliament and honorary lieutenant-colonel; Samuel F. B. Morse; Carl Schmidt; Gustav Stephen; Kaiser Wilhelm II; Frederick Hamilton-Temple-Blackwood (Lord Dufferin), 1st Earl of Dufferin, 1st Marquess of Dufferin and Ava; Rev. G. K. B. Adams (and his Anniversary War Service address, which appears in a modified form); King George V; the Fifty-Second Battalion black bear cub mascot; the Twirling Talbuts; racehorses Wilkmer, King Okla, and Lady May; and the Blackstone Quartette.

Please see the back of the book for historical information (p. 275), photographs (p. 287), and a glossary of Finnish words with a basic pronunciation guide (p. 282).

Well, there is no shallow water, and naught but love to keep
Us safely from the dangers and the devils of the deep
Yet with every breath within us we search forevermore
To find some peaceful harbor on that far-off shore

—BILL STAINES, "Crossing the Water"

CHAPTER 1 | Saara

"A great English journalist has confessed that he does not know when the war will end. There used to be quite a number of men on the street who could tell, but they are not so numerous now."—The Note Book, column in *Port Arthur Daily News*, 1915

"EXTRA! EXTRA!" barked John, slamming the front door and bursting into the kitchen. Switching to the language our family used—Finnish—he said, "Somebody tried to burn down the *Daily News* building!"

With a gasp, Mama dropped her wooden spoon in the porridge pot.

Hold on, Saara, I told myself. Was this another of my brother's pranks? No, John actually reeked of smoke!

"What happened?" demanded Papa, lowering that morning's *Port Arthur Daily News*.

"Fred and I were first to pick up our newspapers at the back this morning," said John, still panting from running uphill, "and we saw flames leaping from a stack of papers."

"Why would someone want to destroy the *Daily News* building?" I asked. "All the paper prints is boring reports about the war." There were days while helping Aunt Marja at the farm the last three months that I'd forgotten there was even a war on. But after four days back in Port Arthur, I was reminded constantly.

"Maybe it was a German spy," said John, "who doesn't want us to win the war."

A spy? I doubted that could be true. I circled the table, setting out our bowls.

"Was anyone hurt?" asked Mama.

"No—they put out the fire while it was small. So we still had plenty of papers to sell."

"And today's paper finally has some good war news," said Papa. "Canadians fought marvellously, according to Carrick."

I stared at the front page. The war between our Allied forces—mainly Russia, France, and the British Empire, including Canada—and Germany had already lasted eleven months. *GRIPPING STORY OF WAR OPERATIONS ... STUPENDOUS CONFLICTS ARE BREWING ... GREAT GALLANTRY OF CANADIAN OFFICERS GETS RECOGNITION ...* these were only a few of the war-related headlines.

"Jussi," said Mama, wrinkling her nose at my brother, "I can't believe you sold newspapers in those vile clothes. Go upstairs and get yourself out of them now." She returned to stirring the porridge. "Then add them to what's soaking in the boiler so Saara can wash them."

My jaw dropped. "But I have to see Principal Graham at nine o'clock—"

"Now that you're back home," said Papa, "we expect you to help with chores."

"You must be in BIG trouble with Mr. Graham," taunted John.

"I am *not* in trouble."

"Isn't school over, Saara?" asked Mama.

"Yes—I only need to pick up my report card. With me away the past few months, and Mr. Graham having two classes to look after, he just forgot to write mine, that's all." My Junior Fourth teacher, Miss Rodgers, had left for Toronto in mid-June to care for her brother. He was wounded in France fighting at Ypres. Mr. Graham thought I'd left school entirely, not just until Auntie was well.

"Jussi, where is your report card?" asked Papa. "I didn't see it here on the table when I got home from my meeting last night."

I scoffed, "It must be so bad you're ashamed to show it."

"It's in the parlour and it's fine," said John, sticking his tongue out at me. As he went to fetch his report card he muttered, "But I bet you failed 'cause you missed the examinations."

No, Mr. Graham wouldn't fail me. My grades were excellent ... until March, that is. I hadn't attended school since then. And the examinations *were* important. What if Mr. Graham would not allow me to advance into Senior Fourth come September? My pulse quickened at that horrible thought. Now I had to wait until nine o'clock to find out his decision.

"Seeing Mr. Graham won't take all day," said Mama. "You can do the washing and ironing when you come home so I can get my sewing work done."

John handed his report card to Papa, then headed upstairs to change. I carried on with brewing my Red Rose tea and setting the breakfast table, fully expecting Papa to scowl over John's report. Instead he nodded, saying, "Some improvement. Good for Jussi."

Was my little brother finally starting to take school seriously?

"SAARA!" hollered John as he flew down the stairs. In English he yelled, "A dog chased Sipu up a tree!" Rounding the corner into the kitchen, he blurted, "She's stuck in the poplar meowing and hissing!"

I plunked the milk bottle on the table.

"It's only a cat," grumbled Papa.

"Quick, Saara—she needs your help!" urged my brother.

"*Mitä ihmettä?*" asked Mama, glancing up from spooning the porridge into our bowls.

There was no time for me to translate for her. Papa would have to explain what had happened. Down the hallway I sprinted, my dress flapping against my bare legs.

I raced through the enclosed porch, out the door, and into a head-on collision with the letter carrier. He kept his grip on the stack of envelopes in his hand, but his cap toppled to the ground.

"Hall-o! Have a fire in there, miss?"

"I have to rescue my cat," I said, pointing to the treetop.

The letter carrier looked upward to the branches and chuckled. "Well, I'll be jiggered!" He retrieved his cap and slapped off the dust. "Since when does a wee kitty chatter like a squirrel?"

My cheeks felt on fire. Sure enough, the only tail up that tree was three times as bushy as Sipu's.

"Here's your mail, miss." He repositioned his mailbag, slung crosswise from his right shoulder.

"Thank you. I … I'm sorry for crashing into you."

"No harm done, miss." The letter carrier smiled and touched the brim of his cap in farewell. "Good morning to you."

My brother was watching through the porch window. "Honest, Saara," he said, seeming genuine, "Sipu was up there meowing. She must have got down herself."

I needed that tea to settle me. In the kitchen, I handed the two envelopes to Mama, then poured myself a cup of steaming orange pekoe.

"More bills to pay," said Mama, frowning. "Why such a hurry to get the mail, Saara?"

Before I could get a word out, John piped up. "She's hoping to hear from Mikko." He batted his eyelashes and pretended to swoon.

Brothers! He was right, but I would never admit it out loud. Mikko lived in North Branch. His cousin Lila, who lived near my aunt and uncle, had introduced us. Mikko and I had become friends during my stay at the farm.

I took my place at the table. Before I even reached for the sugar bowl, John handed it to me. Why was he being kind to me? What did he want? *Never mind.* I smiled at him. Perhaps he'd changed while I'd been away. I added a heaping spoonful of sugar to my tea, topped it up with milk, and stirred it well.

"I'll be out longer tomorrow morning," said John, grinning. "I've got a delivery route now!"

"How did you manage that?" said Papa. "You've been asking for one for months."

"Yesterday the carrier boy fell off the playground sliding board. He busted both his wrists. So they asked me to take over his route."

"The poor boy," said Mama. "It will be weeks before he's healed."

"Maybe I'll have his route all summer!" exclaimed John. When Mama gave him a disapproving look, he changed his tune. "It *is* too bad for him, all right."

"Where is your route, Jussi?" asked Mama.

"Up near Prospect School and the government wireless station."

"What about hawking papers on the street corner?" said Papa.

"I'll still be able to do that first thing. Then I'll deliver papers to the houses on my route."

Picking up my cup of tea, I blew across the surface. Then I took a sip … and gagged! Instead of sweet, my tea was salty—*extremely* salty. I spewed it clear across the table. Milky tea sprayed Papa's newspaper. John grinned at me. Yes, he'd changed—for the worse! He had obviously filled the sugar bowl with salt.

Papa flung the newspaper to the floor and bellowed,

"Saara, that was inexcusable. Go to your bedroom."

I hadn't eaten even one mouthful of my porridge. On my way past John, he gloated and whispered, "April Fool's times two!"

Why times two? Did he mean Sipu? So my cat hadn't been in trouble after all. What a little actor John had become. I clenched my fists to keep from smacking his head, "You're three months late," I hissed.

"You were away then, so you missed out on the fun. Lighten up!"

"Don't be so immature, John."

"Saara, upstairs, now!" ordered Papa.

I stomped off, wishing I'd already put on my shoes. Stomping in one's bare feet was most unsatisfying.

At the door to my bedroom I stopped. A furry grey ball was curled beside my pillow. "Sipu, here you were asleep all along when I was coming to your rescue." She stood, arched her back, and stretched her front legs.

I plopped onto my yellow patchwork quilt beside my cat. "John is such a pest! A nuisance! A TRIAL! That's what a brother is." I punched my pillow. Sipu twitched the tip of her tail and scurried out of my bedroom. She knew when it was best to leave me alone. Too bad John didn't have her sense.

I couldn't believe I'd actually missed my brother while I was living at the farm. How could I have forgotten his annoying habits and incessant pranks? He'd never been more irritating than since I'd come back home. He had a knack for bringing out my worst behaviour even when I was determined not to let him affect me.

Papa left for work. Down the hall from my bedroom, Mama was treadling her sewing machine.

"Mama, I'm going to Fred's house," yelled John from the bottom of the stairs.

"All right, but I'll be calling you home in an hour," she replied.

John banged the porch door on his way out. Fred's family was Ukrainian, and since they'd moved in next door three years ago, he and John had been friends.

After rebraiding my hair for the day, I returned to the kitchen. It was quarter past eight. There was still time to have breakfast, yet I didn't feel like eating a lot. My stomach was in a flutter over what Mr. Graham would say.

What a relief that Mama hadn't saved my porridge for me—or my ruined tea. She never threw out leftover food, even with Papa working full-time, so someone else must have eaten it. Instead I sliced the rye bread—expertly, after all my homemaking experience at the farm— and buttered a piece. Better than everyday porridge, especially when it's gone cold. Thankfully, Mama had left the teapot on the wood stove to keep warm. I poured a fresh cup, sweetened it with a lump of Papa's sugar, and added milk.

I sat down to my meal and reached for the newspaper to distract me. It was now missing the tea-splattered front page. I turned to page four, past all the war news, to find the editor's quips in The Note Book. They were usually matter-of-fact or thoughtful, and some gems made me laugh. Unfortunately there were no funny ones today.

"SAARA!" shouted John from the porch.

"Go away! I'm not falling for your pranks anymore."

"This ain't a joke."

"*Isn't* a joke."

"Quit the grammar lesson and come here!" he snapped.

He did sound worried. Either John was truly becoming a skilled actor, or this was truly urgent. I wasn't ready to believe him yet. I picked up my bread and strolled to the porch.

"What now, pest?"

John looked stricken as he dragged me outside. Pointing next door, he said, "The police are at Fred's house!"

CHAPTER 2 | John

"Germany now claims to have 1,000,000 prisoners of war."—The Note Book, *Port Arthur Daily News,* 1915

Me and Fred was playing soldiers, digging a trench like they're doing in France. Then a big black police patrol wagon rolled into our side lane. It parked right in front of Fred's house. We dropped our shovels and ran over. I ain't never seen one so up close before. Bold white letters on the side spelled "POLICE PATROL."

The officers jumped out. One of them said, "Which of you boys lives here?"

"I do," said Fred.

"Is your father at home?"

"Yes, he is." He gave me a puzzled look.

"We need to talk to him."

Now Fred looked scared stiff. But he remembered how to move his legs and took the officers inside his house.

I ran to fetch Saara. She took a whole bunch of convincing to come outside.

Now she stared at the patrol wagon with wide eyes. "Why are they here?" she asked.

"I don't know," I said with a shrug. My hands trembled.

I shoved them quick in my knickers pockets. "They've been inside a long time." I gulped a breath. My eyes watered. I fought back tears.

The front door of the house opened. We heard a high-pitched cry.

"Oy, no take him! He no do wrong," bawled Fred's mother. She was weeping.

Two policemen marched Fred's father to the back of the patrol wagon. They loaded him inside. One slammed the door and locked it tight. Then he pulled himself up onto the rear platform. The other officer started the engine. The black truck roared off along our short side lane toward Foley Street. Fred's mother picked up her skirts and ran after it. She was wailing the whole way. The cop clinging to the pole at the back never looked at her. She didn't stop chasing the patrol wagon until it turned onto Foley and drove downhill.

"Why'd they arrest him, Saara?" I asked. "What'll they do with him?"

"I have no idea," she said. "We'll tell Papa what happened and he'll find out."

Fred's mother was returning. Most of her hair was loose from her bun. She was sobbing and gulping air.

"We need to get Mama," said Saara.

We rushed inside our house.

Mama was watching from the parlour window. She must have heard the commotion. Her fingers twisted the hem of her apron. She said, "I was hoping the rumours had no truth."

"What rumours?" asked Saara.

Mama kept staring out the window, not answering.

"You might as well say it, Mama. John and I will find out soon enough."

Mama took a deep breath. "I heard that married men, not just single immigrant men, have been sent away to the 'internment camp.'" She used the English name.

"What *is* an 'internment camp'?" asked Saara. "Why are they sending people there?"

"Would they send Papa away, too?" I said.

"No, Jussi." Mama slipped her arm around me. "Only the foreigners they call 'enemy aliens.' Germans, Austro-Hungarians, including Ukrainians—"

"Like Fred's family," I said. "But Fred's my friend and his father is a good person. They're not our *enemies*."

"I know, Jussi," said Mama. "But in wartime, people are suspicious."

"Where is the camp?" asked Saara.

"Eastern Ontario, at Kapuskasing."

I brushed away a leaked tear with my sleeve. "How long will Fred's father be gone?"

"Only God and the government know. But my guess is for as long as the war lasts." Mama untied her apron and handed it to Saara. "I'll see what help I can be next door."

I had lots more questions, but they'd have to wait till later. Mama wasted no time getting over there. I wondered if Fred's mother'd quit crying yet.

Saara nibbled her bread. I started playing solitaire. It wasn't enough to take my mind off what'd happened. I kept thinking about Fred's father. Stacking the cards, I asked, "What's 'interment' mean?"

"In*tern*ment."

Why did Saara *always* have to correct me? She knew what I was trying to say. "Fine, *teacher*—but what does it mean?"

"I don't know. Look it up."

I fetched the dictionary from the parlour and set it on the kitchen table. Flipping the pages back and forth, I looked up the word. There was no *internment,* but I found *intern.* Underlining the words with my finger, I read aloud, "'Intern: to confine or impound.'"

"I guess they just want to keep the enemy aliens in one place," said Saara.

We heard the front door open. Then Mama showed up in the kitchen doorway.

"Is Fred's father really going to the 'internment camp'?" I asked, again using English for those frightening two words. My heart was drumming a tattoo inside my chest.

"Yes, that's what I understand from Fred's mother," said Mama. She sounded sad. "I'll ask Papa to make sure her name is added to the list to get relief funds from the government. Well, I must get back to my sewing now."

"And I better go find Fred." I made my way outside. *What do you say to a fellow who just had his father hauled away by the cops?* For sure he needed cheering up. *A good wrestling match and a few jokes should do the trick.*

CHAPTER 3 | Saara

"It's easier to stand up and meet hard luck face to face than it is to dodge it."—The Note Book, *Port Arthur Daily News*, 1915

I tossed my braids over my shoulders and checked the parlour clock. The hands showed quarter to nine; it was time for me to go see Mr. Graham. I dreaded getting my report card if it contained the words "Saara must repeat Junior Fourth." But that was *not* going to happen. I squared my shoulders to boost my confidence and then walked the four blocks to South Ward Public School.

Inside Mr. Graham's office, I perched on the hard edge of the wooden chair. He was frowning and going *hmm, hmm* as he rustled papers. I hoped it wasn't because of me that he didn't look pleased.

He picked up his pencil, stood, and faced the wall calendar. Using his pencil tip, he counted dates. I ordered myself to relax, but myself didn't listen. Pressing my palms hard on my thighs didn't stop my legs from quaking.

Mr. Graham turned to look at me. He said nothing.

Finally he spoke. "Miss Mäki, I see that you have

missed seventy-one days of school. How exactly were you helping your relatives in North Branch?"

"I cared for my baby cousin, sir, and cooked and cleaned. You see, my aunt was contagious, fighting tuberculosis. It was stubborn, but Auntie won her battle and then I could come home."

Mr. Graham shook his head. "Still, that is a significant amount of lost time."

"It wasn't all lost, sir. I took work along, and I taught English to my friend and her cousin." My "classes" with Lila and Mikko were not as frequent—or as polished—as I'd hoped, but my students *had* made progress.

"That doesn't make up for lost instruction, I'm afraid. Besides, you missed the promotion examinations."

"Please let me write the examinations, sir, so I can go into Senior Fourth."

"That is impossible. The examinations were set by the district. I cannot give you the opportunity to cheat by consulting your fellow students."

"I promise I won't cheat, sir."

"No, I've made my decision. As admirable as it was for you to help your relatives, you have failed Junior Fourth and will have to repeat the year."

No! I struggled to keep from bursting into tears. "Can you please use my marks up until March? I got the highest grades in everything except mathematics."

Mr. Graham arched his eyebrows and picked up the papers from his desk. "These are notes from your former teacher, Miss Rodgers. She does indicate here that you were one of her top students." His voice sounded grudging. He tapped his pencil eraser against the papers, then cleared his throat. "The only way to compensate for the time lost is to complete special assignments in a comprehensive manner."

For the first time since I entered his office, I felt hopeful. "I'll do whatever you ask, sir." I gulped. "I want to become a qualified teacher."

Mr. Graham's already sombre expression grew more stern. "Wait by my secretary's desk while I prepare your assignments."

I slipped out of his office, closed the door, and sat down to wait. The longer I stared at the minute hand on the wall clock, the slower it seemed to move.

After fifteen agonizing minutes, Mr. Graham emerged. He handed me the homework sheets, textbooks, foolscap for practice writing, and a scribbler for good copy. "Turn in your work to me on or before July 15. Then in August you will receive a letter from me with your results."

"Yes, sir."

"Be warned: I will not tolerate lateness, and I expect your work to be excellent."

"I will do my best work."

"Miss Mäki, should I decide you must repeat Junior Fourth, that could disqualify you from teacher's training."

All the way home, the principal's warning rang in my ears. I scanned the pages he'd prepared. Lots of mathematics equations and a few problems; scores of grammar exercises; three composition topics; and an essay. There was so much work to do! Panic squeezed my lungs. How would I finish it all?

You can do this, Saara. You have no choice.

Turning from Secord Street up the back lane, I planned my day. If I swiftly dealt with the laundry, I could get some of the grammar questions done this afternoon.

I found Mama on the porch steps calling my brother home.

"What's all that you're carrying?" asked Mama, leading the way to the kitchen. "I thought you were getting your report card."

"I won't get it until after I finish these assignments. And I have only two weeks to get them all done! If my work isn't good enough, I might have to repeat Junior Fourth." I plunked the stack on the table.

"Well, Saara," said Mama, stroking my hair, "Papa and I knew when we agreed you could go to the farm that there might be such a price to pay. That is life. Taking longer to finish school is not the end of the world."

That's fine for you to say—it could be the end of my dream!

She continued, "'Commit your work to the Lord, and your thoughts will be established.'"

"Is that a Finnish proverb?"

"No—that one is from the Bible."

Thinking of all the work ahead of me, I prayed silently, *I commit this to you, God. Please help me do well.*

John rushed into the house, asking, "What do you want?"

Mama rinsed her coffee cup and set it in the sink. She patted a brown-paper-wrapped package on the table. "Mrs. Brooks will have her dress in time for the Dominion

Day festivities, as requested. After you two deliver it to her, you can pick up the groceries."

"But what about all of this?" I said, pointing to my homework. John glanced at my stack and snickered.

"You'll need to get it done after your chores," said Mama, adding another item to the shopping list.

Then my brain caught up to her earlier words. "Why us *two*? I don't need John's help." No John = No Pranks + Peace. Now that was arithmetic I liked.

"I don't want to run errands anyway," groused John.

"I can do the shopping on my own, Mama," I said.

"I have no doubt, Saara. Jussi could manage it by himself, too. But it's the lugging uphill that requires the strength of both of you. The list isn't long, but there are some heavy items. You'll need the handcart."

I sighed. John heaved a bigger sigh.

Removing the lid of her coffee-tin bank, Mama counted out coins. "Prices keep going up, but this should be enough, together with the payment from Mrs. Brooks," she said, handing the money to me.

I slipped the cash into my Coca-Cola coin purse. I returned it to my dress pocket along with the list. The purse had been a thoughtful birthday gift from John shortly after the ship we were on, the *Empress of Ireland*, sank just over one year ago. I felt a twinge of guilt for saying I didn't need John's help. But anger quickly replaced the guilt when I remembered the shock of salty tea and the shame of splattering Papa's newspaper.

"Let's go, brat," I said, grabbing the package and heading outside. *God, please don't let him embarrass me.*

"Only 'cause Mama says I have to," said John, following me and slamming the porch door behind him. "Bossy," he added, sticking out his tongue.

"Careful, or I'll salt your tongue," I said, placing the package in the two-wheeled handcart and picking up the right-side handle. He laughed. Maybe he realized I meant business because without arguing he grabbed the other handle and helped pull the handcart.

Already the sun was scorching the weeds down the middle of the dirt back lane. By the time we passed my best friend Helena Pekkonen's house, my cotton dress was damp. How I longed for a breeze off Lake Superior.

Opposite the Co-Op grocery store, I said, "Let's park the handcart over there. Then we don't have to bring it to Mrs. Brooks's house." We crossed Secord Street.

"It ain't safe to leave it," said John.

"Who'd steal a rickety old cart like ours?"

"Spies, to carry their dynamite."

"That's ridiculous. There aren't any spies around here." John picked up a lot of local gossip while on duty selling newspapers. Less than half of it was true, I was sure.

"Sabotagers was in Nipigon this spring to blow up the Canadian Pacific Railway bridge," said John.

"*Saboteurs were*, and nothing has been proven in court, has it?"

"Not yet. But they did have a fuse and loaded revolvers." He shook his head, saying, "No, it ain't safe. There's been lots of thieving around town, too, with so many men out of work."

"We'd only need to worry if it was loaded with food," I said.

He aimed his finger at me. "If it disappears while we're gone, it's *your* fault."

"Okay, okay. We'll bring it along." I reached for my handle, then stopped. "Or you could wait with it here. I can be there and back within twenty minutes."

"I'll stay put."

Carrying the package, I hoofed it the three blocks along Secord Street, envying John getting to rest in the shade. Mrs. Brooks's domestic came to the door when I knocked. The girl didn't look a day over fourteen—closer to thirteen, like me—yet dark bags puffed below her eyes.

"Hello. I have a delivery for Mrs. Brooks."

"All right, I'll take it," she said, reaching for the package.

I pulled back. "Usually I give it to her directly and she provides payment."

"Suit yourself. Who do I say is here?"

"Saara Mäki."

"Saara? Is that you, dear?" called Mrs. Brooks from the gloomy interior. "For heaven's sake, do come in. Mimi, you may return to the baking."

"Yes, ma'am," said Mimi with an awkward curtsy.

Mrs. Brooks tut-tutted. "This new girl requires far more training than I'm accustomed to providing. You have my altered dress, I presume?"

"Yes, Mrs. Brooks." I handed her the package. In return she gave me a packet of money.

"Have you now finished housekeeping for your aunt?"

"Yes. I moved back home last Friday. My aunt is feeling heaps better."

"That is wonderful news, dear," she said, unwrapping the dress and inspecting the stitches of the shortened hem. "Do thank your mother for her precise work once again. Good day."

"You're welcome. Goodbye." I hurried back to the Co-Op. From half a block away I spied the handcart, but there was no sign of John.

CHAPTER 4 | John

"Have you noticed how often men write to newspapers to chide other men for lack of backbone, and then sign fictitious names?"—The Note Book, *Port Arthur Daily News*, 1915

As the Co-Op clerk reached for a tin of coffee, I thought, *I ain't gonna put up with this Sassy Saara treatment anymore. She thinks after three months away she can just prance back to Port Arthur and take over as Big Sister like always, ordering me around. Well, I learned a thing or two while she was gone. For instance, I like telling myself what to do.*

The door flew open and Saara stormed inside. "Oh, there you are. I thought you'd taken off."

"Nope—just got bored," I said. "Did I forget anything?"

Stacked on the counter was the tin of coffee, a sack of oats and a sack of sugar, a peck of potatoes, yeast cakes, a bunch of carrots, and a bunch of beets.

Saara pulled the slip of paper from her dress pocket. She read over the list and eyed the counter. "Yes, you missed an item."

Only one! I grinned.

Saara faced the clerk and said, "We need Sunlight soap, please." He fetched a package.

I couldn't help boasting. "Did good, didn't I, Saara?"

"We'd better pay before the handcart walks off," was all she said.

The clerk punched the prices into the cash register. Saara frowned. Didn't we have enough money? Coffee cost more than the last time I'd bought it.

"Your total is three dollars and forty-five cents," said the clerk.

Saara emptied her coin purse (the one *I* gave her) onto the counter. She opened Mrs. Brooks's packet and poured out the money. Counting it, she said, "Oh, no." Her cheeks flushed. "We're ten cents short. We'll have to leave the yeast cakes or the soap."

"We don't need the soap," I suggested.

Saara glared at me, then told the clerk, "We won't take the yeast cakes."

"I bet Mama still has a part-cake of soap," I reasoned. "But if she ain't got yeast, she can't bake anything." I had a good argument, and I knew she knew it.

"Fine, we'll leave the soap," she huffed.

The clerk moved the package aside. Saara slid the cash toward him. He said thank you and slotted our money into the cash register.

Me and Saara hoisted our purchases outside. After the cool of the store, the day felt extra warm. We began packing the handcart.

"Move the potatoes," Saara ordered. "The sugar has to go in that spot."

There she goes, bossing me again. "Does not. It should go in the centre to balance the load."

It looked like she was about to snap back at me. But all she did was mutter "Drat" under her breath. Ha! I was right—*again.*

We grabbed the handles and rolled the cart onto Secord Street to cross over. A block away, a horse pulling a wagon was trotting toward us. We was doing fine until the cart's wheels got stuck in a rut. That made us strain harder. I grunted and tugged. We finally hauled the wheels clear. But the wagon was closing in on us.

"We have to go faster, John," wheezed Saara.

"Let down your side."

"I can't go any lower—I'm too tall."

"You can so!"

"Can't!" she puffed. "Hold your side up more, weakling."

"Slow down a bit!"

The horse and wagon was about twenty yards away and coming fast.

"Stop flapping your lips and pull harder," demanded Saara.

I'll show her how hard I can pull. I yanked my handle forward and up. The potatoes shifted and half of them tipped out onto the ground. The largest spuds kept rolling.

The horse shied, sidestepping as potatoes bounced toward it. "Get off the road!" shouted the wagon driver. He fought to control his horse.

One of the men standing outside the Coca-Cola bottling works tossed his cigarette and ran toward us. He scooped most of the fallen potatoes into the cart. Then he helped us haul it safely out of the way.

Just in time. The horse and wagon passed the spot where we'd been. The wagon's big wheels left squashed spuds behind on the road.

"Thank you, mister," I said.

"Yer mighty welcome." He reorganized the groceries. "'Tis a waste for quality foodstuffs to get trampled."

"Joseph!" boomed a large man puffing on a cigar. "Are ye done yer good deed for the enemy aliens? 'Tis time we were off."

I stretched as tall as a nine-and-two-thirds-year-old fellow could stand. "We're not enemy aliens," I said loudly to Cigar Man. "We're Finlanders. Me and her was even born in Canada." Yup, we was foreigners. But the acceptable kind—so far.

"John, be quiet," whispered Saara. "Let's get going."

Joseph smiled at us. "Me brother tends toward exaggeration. He sees a girl in pigtails and assumes she's German. Pay him no mind. So long." He waved as he led his brother away.

Cigar Man had more to say, calling out, "Can't be too careful 'bout the enemy."

Me and Saara slogged up the hill, dragging the cart behind us.

The last thing I felt like doing when we reached home was unloading the groceries. But at least I could cool off a bit by going into the basement. Before Saara could start giving me orders, I grabbed the spuds. "I'll carry the vegetables to the cold cellar."

"Fine with me," said Saara. She hefted the sack of oats and stepped inside the porch.

By the end, we was dripping sweat. We sat across from each other at the kitchen table drinking water.

"Thank you both for your hard work," said Mama. She poured herself a cup of coffee and joined us. "Did you put the change in the coffee-tin bank?"

"There wasn't any," said Saara, "and I'll have to go back for soap."

"So expensive," said Mama, sighing. "If only I'd had time to plant a garden. Then we wouldn't have to pay for vegetables all summer and we'd have more money for other needs."

"I can get the soap tomorrow after I sell my papers," I offered.

"No," said my sister, raising her voice. "*I* was responsible for the money and *I* said I would do it."

Why does she have to be so touchy? I kicked her foot. "Mama asked us *both* to do the shopping, and I'm going right past the store—"

"Enough squabbling, you two," said Mama. "No need to make a special trip. I'll start a new grocery list." She muttered to herself, "I miss the peace we had around here when Saara was away."

I knew who'd disturbed the peace since Saara came back, and it wasn't me.

CHAPTER 5 | Saara

"This is the growing season for everything except pay rolls."—The Note Book, *Port Arthur Daily News*, 1915

I knew who'd disturbed the peace since I'd come back—his name was John. *God, please do something about him!* Now the laundry was calling my name.

"I stoked the wood stove a while ago," said Mama, "so the boiler should be hot by now."

"Thank you," I said, adding laundry soap to the heated water. Firmly gripping the handle of the washing plunger, I pushed and pulled it through the water, agitating the clothes.

"Before you start the ironing, you need to deal with that," said Mama, pointing to the mountain of rhubarb in the sink. "Helena brought it over while you were out. They have a bumper crop this year. I need you to stew it today." She headed back upstairs to her sewing machine.

With the long stick, I fished the laundry from the boiler to rinse.

"I'm going to find Fred," said John.

"Good, I got my wish—peace at last," I said, agitating

Papa's trousers and John's knickers and shirts in the rinse water. After feeding them through the wringer, I carried them out the back door and pegged them to the clothesline.

While the irons heated on the wood stove, I washed and chopped the rhubarb. Then I set it to stew and confronted yesterday's mountain of wrinkled laundry. My shoulders sagged. If I scorched a shirt, Mama would have a conniption fit. I took pains to be careful with the ironing, working steadily until my stomach demanded food.

After lunch, I managed to get through the rest of the ironing, can the rhubarb, complete a few grammar questions, and start cooking supper by the time Mama quit sewing for the day.

"To think," she said, "a year ago you could barely cook potatoes, let alone an entire meal." She patted my shoulder, looking pleased. "What a lot you've learned."

Mama's praise grew a joy-bubble inside me. Even Papa's discouraged face when he arrived home from work didn't make it pop.

He slumped into his chair at the kitchen table. "Just when we've got close to our down payment for a house saved, the company cut our wages today," he said. "That's the trouble with a non-union job. If we had a union, this wouldn't have happened."

John came inside for supper. Papa was so busy listing the benefits of a union, he didn't ask him about his day, as usual.

"Fred's father—" John began, but Mama shushed him.

"Later," she whispered.

Hearing my father rant about labour issues brought back a familiar spasm of fear inside me. The last time Papa had gotten riled up about working conditions, he'd gone on strike and lost his job. But God had answered my prayers then and provided for us. Even when it took a whole year for Papa to get a steady job. It was time to pray some more.

Mama poured coffee for him. "I'm thankful you still have full-time work."

Also, unlike poor Fred, our father was still at home.

CHAPTER 6 | John

"The Germans had arranged to blow up the Welland canal at a total cost of $1,000."—The Note Book, *Daily News-Chronicle*, 1916

Me and Fred aimed to be first in line to pick up our papers every morning. So as soon as my Big Ben alarm clock started clanging, I shut it off. It ain't the easiest thing getting up at dawn, but first to get papers means we're first to pick our corners to sell 'em. You need a good corner. Not just lots of people, but plenty of buyers. I'm nowheres close to the best scrapper—too puny—so fighting for the best corner ain't an option.

I pulled·on my shirt, knickers, and socks. With my bootlaces double knotted, I dashed downstairs. I grabbed the thick heel of yesterday's bread to gnaw along the way.

For once, Fred wasn't already outside waiting for me. I knocked, quiet at first, then louder.

Finally he showed up, rubbing his eyes. "I'm gonna have to learn to get myself up. My father always woke me—" His voice croaked. This was his first morning without his father. Then he elbowed my arm. "Come on, slowpoke Johnny," he said, breaking into a run.

I chased him along our side lane. At Foley Street, we turned downhill. That's where we picked up speed. I swung my arms and kicked my legs. Fred still had the lead, but not for long! Just before Secord Street, I caught up and passed him with a loud cheer. Then we slowed to a jog. We had a whole bunch more blocks to go to Lorne Street.

There wasn't many people out yet. Only a couple wagons passed us. We rounded the corner into the lane behind the *Port Arthur Daily News* building. No other newsboys in sight. *Huzzah!*

I spotted Hank Cameron, the *Daily News* reporter. He was the fellow wearing a jaunty cap and hopping into his motorcar. "I'll see what more I can learn from the police," he called to the man at the back door. Mr. Cameron started the engine.

I sprinted to the side of his motorcar. "What's the scoop, Mr. Cameron?"

He stuck his head out the window, saying, "Morning, Johnny," but he forgot his usual smile and wink. Today's news had to be grim. He said, "Sabotage at the wireless station last night."

"Whoa—that *is* big. Can I come with you, Mr. Cameron?"

"Sorry, Johnny, you can't." He reached out his hand and tapped my chest. "I report, you sell the papers."

I slouched, staring at the ground. I'd been a newsboy since before Easter. A couple months back I started practising writing my own reports. Filled half a scribbler so far. How was I going to learn to be a reporter if I couldn't see how Mr. Cameron gathered the facts?

His large hand messed my hair. I glanced up in time to catch Mr. Cameron's grin and wink.

"What you *can* do is call me Cam from now on." With that he grabbed the steering wheel and roared off down the lane.

"You sure got guts, pal," said Fred, punching my shoulder. "Hey, isn't your new paper route up near the wireless station?"

"Yup. It goes right past."

"Maybe you'll see what they wrecked."

As each newsboy showed up, we told him the sabotage news. The last fellow got bombarded with a dozen of us shouting at once. Shoving turned into wrestling. That stopped as soon as the first stacks of newspapers got heaved out the back door.

Me and Fred each paid for a sheaf of papers and took off at a good clip. At my favourite corner, I quickly read Cam's report. Then I started bellowing, "*SABOTAGE! BOLD ATTACK ON PORT ARTHUR WIRELESS STATION!*"

Men in suits and labourers in work clothes came running. Some was so anxious to read the news, they didn't wait for their change. Of course, I was too busy selling papers to run after them. More tips for me! I sold all of my papers in record time and ran back for more. I figured my new route customers could wait a bit longer.

My second batch of papers flew out of my hands just as fast as the first. This was bully! I sure wished I had time to grab another sheaf, but I really had to make my deliveries. There wasn't even time to stop in at my regular businesses today.

After picking up my route papers, I bought one more copy. I lugged the stack over to Red River Road and climbed on the streetcar going uphill. When I caught the conductor's eye, I waved the spare newspaper. The big Finnish man tipped his cap to me and reached for the paper. My fare was paid.

It felt good to sit down and have the streetcar carry me and my load up the long hill. I pulled out the list of addresses and planned my route. At the stop closest to Prospect Avenue, I jumped off. The starting address of my route was near Prospect School. Checking my list, I found each house and dropped off a newspaper.

My heart pounded louder and louder in my ears the closer I got to the wireless station. Cam had written that the sabotagers fired their revolvers before they ran off. What if they was still in the area? *I better be on the lookout.*

Up ahead stood the fence surrounding the station. I couldn't see any damage to the building or the wires and poles. Either the sabotagers didn't wreck much, or it got fixed in a hurry.

I turned to carry on with my route. Sunlight flashed off something on the ground. I moved in for a up-close look. There was a small metal object. It was partly hidden in the grass. I pulled out my handkerchief and used it to pick up the tube. I couldn't believe my eyes. I'd seen a picture of one of these in a library book last week. I felt like I was about to explode—I couldn't wait to tell Fred. I was a hundred and ten percent sure this piece of metal had been inside the sabotager's gun only hours ago!

CHAPTER 7 | Saara

"Canada expects every man and woman these days to do their duty."—The Note Book, *Port Arthur Daily News*, 1915

"Per-spic-u-ity? What is that?" I muttered as I grabbed the dictionary. I flipped my braids onto my back, opened the book to the middle, and hunted for this new word.

"Clearness. Ugh." Why couldn't Mr. Graham have just said to write accurately and clearly? Trust the principal to make the assignment more complicated than it needed to be.

A noble deed is a source of inspiration. Based on this theme, write three pages with accuracy and perspicuity.

I shook my head to unfuddle my brain. My brother's boots clattering down the wooden steps had awakened me at dawn. I thought I might as well make good use of my early rising by diving into my homework. My goal was to get as much as possible done today so I could spend part of tomorrow with Helena at the Dominion Day festivities: swimming, watching the horseback tug-of-war, picnicking. I missed her—we hadn't done anything together since before I left for the farm.

After what seemed like an hour of writing on my foolscap sheets, I heard Mama's footsteps on the stairs.

"Good morning, Saara," she said in her usual Finnish, interrupting my accurate and *perspicuous* English.

"Good morning," I mumbled and kept writing.

Mama turned to the wood stove to make coffee and start cooking porridge. "Do you want tea?" she asked.

"Yes, please." Mama bustled about while I frantically scribbled. I had two ideas buzzing in my head to get down on paper before they evaporated.

A while later Papa came downstairs and checked the front steps for today's *Daily News*. Returning empty-handed, he harrumphed and muttered, "Not here yet," then settled in to read his Finnish newspaper instead. He wasn't talkative this morning, which suited me fine.

Thank goodness I had fully developed my second idea when Mama said, "Jussi isn't here yet, but it's time to eat."

I rushed through breakfast and started clearing the table.

"What's the hurry, Saara?" asked Papa.

"I want to get back to my homework. I need to prove I can do good work quickly, so I can become a teacher."

"Emilia, our daughter wants to be a teacher!" said Papa with a nod of approval. "That's a noble calling."

A noble calling. I smiled. Could I fit that into my composition somehow?

My parents left to do their work. I finished the dishes, then buckled down with my foolscap and pencil.

As I was partway through the last page, Mama reappeared in the kitchen.

"I'm running low on this blue thread," she said, handing me a piece. "I need you to get more right away."

Drat. The errand would take at least an hour. So much for spending all day working on Mr. Graham's assignments. But at least I could sign out the library book I would need to write about Samuel Morse and his invention, the Morse code. I set off at top speed.

"What's this?" I asked, entering the kitchen with Mama's thread and seeing John pasting newspaper articles onto large sheets of manila paper. Thank goodness he'd left my homework undisturbed at the end of the table. "School's over for *you*, John—you can stop doing homework."

"This ain't homework," he crowed. "It's important information to boost the moral of the soldiers."

"*Isn't* homework, and I think you mean *morale*."

"Sure, *teacher*," said John, frowning.

"But how's your scrapbook going to help soldiers?"

"This ain't my scrapbook—it's budget pages. They're going overseas," he said, stacking the manila sheets.

"Budget pages? Isn't a budget a report about money?"

"Ha! Not this kind of budget! Something I know and you don't," he said, bursting with pride. "My teacher got us started making these bundles of news at school. It's something I can do to help the war effort. See, these big papers of clippings get folded and fastened with a cord and then mailed to soldiers." He flipped over the stack to show me where he'd carefully printed "News from Home" and "Port Arthur, Ontario."

"So do you send them all the local news about German spies stealing handcarts to carry their dynamite?" I teased.

"Just 'cause you don't believe there's spies around, doesn't mean there ain't. Look at this," he said, pointing to a clipping on the table. "Just last night sabotagers attacked right here in Port Arthur!"

"You're joking, right?"

He didn't crack a smile. "Nope, I ain't. They tried to wreck the wireless station to stop important communicating."

I looked down and gasped.

SABOTAGE ATTEMPT OF WIRELESS STATION

At about 1:30 o'clock this morning, two men attempted to sabotage the government wireless telegraph station in Port Arthur. The saboteurs severed the ropes that secured the Marconi vertical antenna, causing it to fall and incapacitate the wireless station.

Upon investigation, the superintendent discovered the saboteurs attacking the support cables of the tall masts. Interrupted in their sabotage attempt, the men fired their revolvers and then fled the scene. No injuries were incurred by the staff. The saboteurs remain at large.

Militiamen are now in place guarding the wireless station from further attacks, since it has been shown that there are persons here who would like to see damage done to government property. In getting away after their deed at the wireless station, the guilty ones perhaps escaped the death penalty, the same as would be the fate of others in any attempt to interfere there again or likewise at the grain elevators or other places where troops are on guard; for it must not be forgotten that, although active fighting is not going on in this land, the Dominion of Canada is in a state of war.

An attack right here at home! "They're really on the loose? With loaded guns?"

"I can show you proof of that," John boasted, digging in his knickers pocket. He opened his fist and peeled back the corner of his handkerchief. Nestled inside lay a metal cylinder.

"What's that?"

"The casing from a revolver bullet. From the sabotager's gun. I found it this morning doing my paper route. Exciting, ain't it?"

"No—it's scary. The saboteurs could attack other important buildings. People could get hurt—or killed."

"*Now* do you believe me about spies?" Not waiting for me to reply, he grabbed his paste bottle and budget papers and headed toward the stairs. "Say, can you slice some bread for me?"

"If you take this thread to Mama," I said.

John rolled his eyes but took the spool.

Pulling a sharp knife out of the drawer, I began slicing bread. I hated to admit it, but it looked like John was right, after all. There *were* people here who wanted to sabotage Canada's efforts to fight the war. What would they attack next?

46

"Boo!" shouted John, sneaking up right behind me.

"Ah!" Startled, I jerked my hand. I dropped the knife and jumped backward so it wouldn't stab my foot. "Not funny, John."

But he laughed anyway. "Watch out, Saara. Spies could be anywhere," he said, grinning. He snatched two slices of bread, buttered them, and left the house.

I prepared my own lunch, pushing away thoughts of guns and saboteurs. Instead I thought about Helena. She still hadn't given me an answer about spending Dominion Day together, so I gobbled my food and sped down the hill.

A man was crouching in the shadows in the yard across the back lane from Helena's house. Who was that? What was he doing there? I hesitated, uncertain. Was he a saboteur? The man stood and poured water on the garden. Oh, it was only Mr. Campbell. Boy, did I feel foolish.

I climbed the back steps of Helena's house. Her parents, Finnish immigrants like Mama and Papa, ran a boarding house. After I stepped through the porch and knocked on the inner door, Helena appeared—at least, I thought it was Helena. The unsmiling girl standing in the Pekkonens' kitchen wearing Helena's clothes peered out from behind a pasty mask. Every inch of her face looked like melted candle wax. "What's wrong with your face?" I asked.

"Pimples! I'm horrified," said Helena's voice. "I've used mercolized wax every night for a week and my skin is no clearer. I can't go out in public with you tomorrow, Saara. I'd be the laughingstock of everyone."

"Do you think you should wash it off before it's stuck forever?"

I was joking, but Helena was aghast. She screeched, "Can it do that?" and dashed away.

I said goodbye to the now empty kitchen and left. When we'd first talked about going swimming at Current River Park on Dominion Day, Helena said she might have to help out all day in their boarding house. Then she told me she might spend the day with her beau, Richard. And now that she was free to go, she was ashamed to show her face because of a few blemishes? My heart stung. Pimples wouldn't keep *me* from spending time with my best friend.

As I shut the back gate and set off for home, I waved to Mr. Campbell hoeing his garden.

"Saara," he called, "I haven't seen you in ages."

"I was helping out at my uncle's farm." Mr. Campbell's tabby cat jumped off the fence to greet me. "Hello, Tiger," I said, stroking his orange fur.

"Any time you want to help out with my little farm here, feel free," he said with a chuckle, holding up his hoe.

I laughed, then continued up the back lane. There was plenty to keep me busy with school work and chores.

I was one house away from ours when I heard quick footsteps coming up behind me.

CHAPTER 8 | John

"We hope to see the day when men will be asked only to live for their country."—The Note Book, *Port Arthur Daily News*, 1915

"Saara!" I charged up the back lane after her.

Saara whipped around, looking like she'd had a fright. Then she switched to looking annoyed. I waved a small, black box camera and called, "Look what I bought at the drugstore!"

Her face was all scrunched up as she tried to figure out what I was holding. Then I got close enough for her to see.

"A camera? How could you be so wasteful?" she demanded.

"I'm not wasteful." *Why does she always think the worst about me?*

"Papa just had his wages cut and you throw away money on that?"

"I got a unbelievable deal—half price. It only cost one dollar."

"That's still a lot. What about film? And getting it developed? Mama will never pay for that."

"I'll pay for it with my *own* money."

Saara flinched, then scowled at me. "Why do you want a camera, anyhow?"

"So's I can send some pictures to wounded soldiers in England. There's too much words in newspapers."

On Dominion Day morning, I heard the sewing machine whirring. From the doorway I said, "How come you're working, Mama? It's a holiday."

"Not for me, Jussi," she said, stopping to stretch her back. "I need to finish altering these dresses for Mrs. Entwhistle, and Papa is busy at the Big Finn Hall all day."

"Then how am I going to get to the military tattoo?" I asked. I couldn't keep the whine out of my voice, I was so disappointed. "You promised I could go today."

"I know I did, Jussi," said Mama. "Your sister will have to take you."

Saara appeared, hair all mussed. "Take him where?" she asked, then yawned with her mouth wide open.

"Current River Park."

Before Saara could complain, I asked Mama, "Can Fred come, too?"

"Yes, why don't you take Fred as well, Saara? Give his mother some respite."

Mama wasn't really asking. She was telling Saara she had to. My sister rolled her eyes and said, "At least I get to cool off in the swimming pool. I heard today is going to be a scorcher. But when we get home, I *have* to spend time on my homework."

While Saara packed a picnic lunch, I ran next door to get Fred. We rolled our bathing suits in our towels

(I tucked in my camera, too). Cooling off in the water was okay, but I wasn't so keen on swimming. That scary night when the *Empress* sank and I almost drowned still gave me nightmares. It took me all last summer to grow my courage back for jumping in the swimming pool.

Me and Fred and Saara set out for the electric streetcar. Lots of grown-ups and kids was waiting at the stop. When the streetcar braked, they climbed on board first. Then Saara stepped on 'cause she had all our nickels. As soon as she paid our fare, me and Fred scuttled toward the back to grab a pair of seats. Fred beat me to the window and claimed the best seat with his towel roll. We arm-wrestled sitting down, but the angle wasn't right. So we kneeled on the floor, our elbows on the seat.

Someone stumbled over my feet. I guess they was sticking out in the aisle a bit. I tucked them under me.

I looked up and saw the back of a stocky man. Without turning around, he said, "*Verzeihung.*" Then he moved into the row of seats behind ours, across the aisle. He sure looked serious. I guessed what he said was "Pardon me," but it wasn't in Finnish or Ukrainian or even Italian. Was it German? Was he a spy? I wanted so bad to whisper to Fred, but I didn't dare.

We was almost at our stop near the park. It was roasting in the streetcar. I sneaked a peek across the aisle. Mr. Serious was staring straight ahead. How would a reporter like Cam describe him? He was old—at least thirty. He was clutching his leather knapsack on his lap. Under his light brown fringe, his forehead shone, all sweaty. I wished I could take a photograph.

The streetcar squealed to a standstill. Most of the passengers was getting off. Saara was waiting for us outside with the picnic basket and her sack. Me and Fred grabbed our towel rolls and hopped down to the ground. Was Mr. Serious going to the park, too? I didn't like having him following us. So I dawdled.

The streetcar rumbled away toward the end of the line.

"Come on, Johnny," said Fred, tugging my sleeve. "Time to jump in the pool."

"Hold your horses. I gotta fix my lace." My lace was fine, but I bent down and retied it anyhow.

A family with two little boys passed us. Then an older couple. I just *had* to look back. Mr. Serious was there. But he was walking away from the park, toward Lake Superior. *Dandy.* I let out the breath I was holding. I didn't know where he was going, but I liked that it wasn't with us.

Me and Fred ran and caught up with Saara. She parked our lunch under a shady maple tree, and we climbed up the stairs to the pool deck. Lots and lots of kids was already in the shallow part of the swimming pool. They was splashing and squealing. The gigantic above-ground pool stretched far off to the right. We ducked into the separate dressing rooms to change into our bathing suits.

Me and Fred was ready before my sister. When she stepped out into the bright sunlight, she squinted, trying to spot us.

"Smile, Saara," I said from the pool edge.

"Why?"

I quickly pulled my camera from behind my back. "So you don't break my new camera," I said, snickering. *Click.* "Now you, Fred."

I held my camera steady, staring into the viewfinder on the top. Fred grinned and flexed his arm muscles. *Click.* "My turn now," I said, handing my camera to Fred. Then I did a strong-man pose. *Click.*

Saara wiped the sweat off the side of her face. "Put your camera in a safe place and let's get in the pool," she said.

I ran to the maple tree and tucked my camera in the basket.

Back at the pool edge, I pushed Fred in and jumped after him. Water splashed in every direction.

Saara followed on our heels and shrieked. "It's so cold!" She pinched her nose and plunged under anyhow.

When I stood, the water came up to my chest. For younger kids, it was neck deep. Fred was whooping with some other boys. I plowed through the water to reach them.

A fellow about my age was trying to walk along the flat top of the cement pool wall. It was narrow. He teetered on the far edge. Was he going to tip over? We heard girls screaming. They must be on the ground on the other side of the wall. The guy fell out of our sight. We hustled to the wall to look over. He was fine. It wasn't a long drop to the ground. He scrambled back up onto the wall.

"Let's splash him!" shouted Fred.

We drenched him and the wall until he lost his balance. This time he flopped into the water on our side. We laughed so hard.

"I'm gonna try," said Fred. He climbed up and slipped

off the soaked wall before taking three steps. I lasted only a moment longer "walking the plank." It was way tougher than it looked.

The fellow who'd gone over the wall started a game of tag. It was tough to dodge whoever was "it." The churned-up water looked like a boiling spud pot.

"John! Fred!" called Saara. "Let's eat!"

I didn't answer her. We'd hardly gotten started in the pool.

"I've got the shivers!" yelled Saara, wading closer to us. "Let's towel off and have our lunch."

"You have to catch us first!" I shouted. Then I waved Fred toward the deeper end of the pool and took off.

My sister roared, "You are a Pest with a capital P!" and swam-ran after me.

I veered, but she caught hold of my leg. I spun around and kicked myself free. My flying foot landed a blow to her hip.

"Ow!" she yelped, grimacing.

She had to be faking. It couldn't have hurt that much. I laughed and splashed her hard. Then me and Fred raced away.

"Get back here, you rascal!" she shouted, rushing after us.

Suddenly my arm felt like it was in a vice.

"It's time to go, brat," snapped Saara. "The games are starting soon, and there're things I want to see."

I squirmed out of her clutches, tripped, and plunged underwater. Then I couldn't get up. Something was holding me! I was going to drown!

I panicked and fought like a wild beast. Finally, I twisted free and popped up, sputtering. "Why'd you do that?" I coughed and scowled at her, trying hard not to cry. "Why'd you hold me down?"

I thought she'd say sorry, but then Fred appeared. He gave me a friendly slap on the back. I coughed again.

"Come on," said Saara, "we need to get out of the pool, or we'll miss the horseback tug-of-war and the bayonet exercises."

Me and Fred didn't care about a dumb tug-of-war with horses. But for sure we wanted to see the soldiers practise spearing the enemy. So we climbed out of the pool. The park was filling up with carloads of people. Lots was picnicking.

Pulling on my dry knickers, I patted the left pocket. Yup, the bullet casing was still there. Me and Fred made tracks to the picnic basket. Saara was already there. She handed out ham sandwiches and boiled eggs.

"Thank you," said Fred, taking a huge bite of his sandwich.

I was too mad at Saara to say anything nice. So I ignored her. When I chomped half an egg, my stomach cheered.

We downed our lunch in a flash and found seats in the grandstand. It was packed. I made Fred sit between me and my sister. So much noise! The chattering crowd. Squealing ragtime from the merry-go-round. And on top of that, music from two different bands, the Port Arthur City Band and the Fifty-Second Battalion Band.

I couldn't wait to see the soldiers-in-training battle, even if it was only in fun. Pretty soon these "Port Arthur boys" would be shipping out. They'd take their places in the trenches at the Front in France. What an adventure!

Then I remembered Richard's brother Gordon. He'd turned eighteen last year and was so excited to enlist. But in May, his family got the awfulest telegram. Gordon had been killed in action at Ypres. How many of these new soldiers would make it home from the war?

The Fifty-Second Battalion Band blasted a fanfare. The crowd hushed. We focused on the field. It was time for the horseback tug-of-war. Saara was nutty about anything to do with horses. She smiled at me, but I turned away.

The mounted soldiers lined up their horses. The men gripped the thick rope. Then trouble began. War horses was trained for charging into battle, not having their riders haul backward on a rope. Two horses bolted. Okay, this was more interesting than I thought it would be. One horse even bucked off its rider! The soldier was lucky, though. His horse didn't run far so he could quickly get back in the saddle. The whole audience laughed at the men trying to control their horses. Finally they was all in place and the tug-of-war got going. We all clapped and yelled.

The teams tugged and tugged. Still no winner. Several horses shied. Some whinnied. Some lifted their front feet off the ground. Their riders had to drop the rope to haul on their reins. It was chaos! We laughed till our bellies hurt, then laughed some more. In the end, it looked to me like the team with the most hands on the rope was named the winner.

The horses and riders cleared the field. A long row of soldiers marched forward. They was ready to demonstrate their bayonets. Each rifle had a sharp metal blade on the end that gleamed in the sunlight. I steadied my camera. *Click*. The men in their khaki-coloured uniforms looked determined. They lunged forward. Their bayonets pierced the air at chest level. *Click*. Then, in pairs, they carried out their exercises. They stabbed straw-filled burlap bags tied to wooden frames. Me and Fred perched on the edge of our seats, goggle-eyed. It all looked so real. I felt like I was at the Front. Our soldiers was fighting in close combat with the Germans.

All of a sudden I remembered what was between the streetcar stop and the lake. The Current River railway bridge. What if Mr. Serious was a real sabotager planning to destroy the bridge?

CHAPTER 9 | Saara

"Cross country criminals should soon learn that for them Port Arthur is not a very healthy stopping off place."—The Note Book, *Port Arthur Daily News*, 1915

"Don't forget your raincoat, Jussi," Mama called after John early Friday morning. From the kitchen window, I could see him go tearing down the back lane. He was minus his raincoat. I wondered how many customers would get soggy newspapers today.

"I feel sorry for the injured boy," said Mama, "but what a godsend for Jussi to have this delivery route on top of his regular newspaper sales."

I grumbled, "We won't see any of his extra earnings added to your coffee-tin bank." *They will all be spent on film and pictures.*

"Saara, that's unkind and unfounded," said Mama. "Your brother has been handing over most of his income from the day he became a newsboy."

From my neck up I felt on fire. So he'd been contributing money to the family and I hadn't. Not even John had told me. I decided it was safest not to say anything more.

Mama reached the stairs, then looked at me over her shoulder. "As soon as Jussi gets back, I have a job for you two," she said and continued up to her sewing.

What now, and why *both* of us? Would I never have a day free of John? A day to fully concentrate on my assignments? I'd carefully scheduled the tasks to be sure I'd complete everything in time. How could I succeed if Mama kept giving me more jobs? She thought I had more than enough time to get my homework done. But I might need to stay up late working to keep on track with my schedule.

Irked, I scurried to wash, dry, and stack the breakfast dishes and sweep the floor. At last, I settled at the kitchen table with my homework. I corrected my perspicuous writing and copied it into my scribbler. I couldn't put off mathematics any longer.

The foot of a ladder is 15 feet from the base of a building, and the top reaches a window 36 feet above the base. What is the length of the ladder? I couldn't make sense of this problem. I prayed and waited five whole minutes. Still confused. *How will I ever get all of this work done?*

When my eyes shifted to the next problem, I exclaimed with relief, "I can do *this* one!" *Using squared paper, graph the temperature at 6 p.m. for ten consecutive days.* I darted up to my bedroom to find a piece of squared paper and my bottle of paste. Back at the table, I carefully set up my graph, filling in the dates. Then I glued it into my scribbler.

Next, I pulled out a fresh sheet of foolscap and began the essay Mr. Graham had assigned: *List three virtues learned while assisting your relatives on their farm, and discuss how these virtues are affecting your behaviour.* I remembered the struggle I'd had in deciding whether or not to go. How I had to give up my star role in the school play. Tuberculosis had sapped Aunt Marja's energy and joy in living. Her battle had certainly tested my fortitude, as I'd had to do all of the cooking and laundry. Washing clothes I'd known how to do, but with cooking, I had a lot to learn.

My patience was forced to grow caring for Baby Sanni on my own. And my love for her—I was sure that counted as a virtue. I'd been home for a week now, and I still listened every morning for her snuffling and whimpering. A wave of longing to cuddle my little cousin had me searching for Sipu. There she was, curled up near the wood stove. Cradling my cat brought back memories of Sanni clinging to me, falling asleep against me. My breath caught in my throat as I suddenly grasped how much Aunt Marja had suffered at the sanatorium being separated from her baby. Had my time at the farm even taught me to better understand someone else's feelings?

Another thing I'd learned while helping my aunt and uncle was to listen to my conscience and do the right thing. My conscience was screaming loud and clear that I was being too hard on John. He was three years younger than I, after all. I needed to be more understanding. I knew I should apologize for holding him under in the swimming pool—after our experience on the *Empress of Ireland*, that had been an especially dirty thing to do.

But no matter how much I reasoned, every time he

pulled another prank I sizzled. Maybe I'd learned to be more patient and understanding with other people, but the truth was, I couldn't with John. Somehow he knew exactly what to do or say that would irritate me the most.

When he arrived home an hour later, he tracked mud through the kitchen. On the floor he knew *I* had to clean. Mama was always hounding him, but he kept forgetting to wipe his boots on the doormat.

If that wasn't enough to interrupt my concentration, he then had to spill the breaking news. "The German spies confessed! They were part of the big plot!"

"Which spies and what plot?" With John announcing the headlines I barely needed to read the newspaper anymore.

"Remember Carl Schmidt and Gustav Stephen?"

"No—what did they do?"

"Right, you were at the farm then. They're the ones who planned to blow up the Nipigon River railway bridge in March. They've been in jail ever since. Now they confessed to even more."

John held up today's newspaper and pointed to the article on the front page. "They're part of the gang that dynamited the armoury in Windsor and the plant in Walkerville that makes soldiers' uniforms. There's as many German spies here in Ontario as in England!"

"Now you're exaggerating."

"I ain't," he insisted, shaking his head. "I got to know what's actual in the papers so's I can sell 'em. There's lots more about spies that I ain't bothered to tell you. Like a couple months ago a Canadian Pacific Railway bridge on the border to the United States was dynamited."

"How do you know all the reports are real?"

"Why would a newspaper print things that ain't true?" he asked.

The whirring upstairs stopped and Mama appeared, stretching her arms and back. The Chore Boss had arrived. "When I delivered the dresses to Mrs. Entwhistle, she asked if you two would come to see her today."

"What does she want?" asked John, whining as usual. It was one of the most annoying sounds in the world.

"She didn't say," replied Mama.

I stacked my foolscap sheets and homework pages. The sooner we saw our neighbour, the sooner I could return to my homework. My deadline was still thirteen days away, but now I was even more worried about meeting it. Mrs. Entwhistle was expecting her first child, and her husband had enlisted last month. She could need help with almost anything.

I gritted my teeth, steeling myself for full-blown whining and fussing from my brother. "Come on," I said, pulling John with me. "We might as well find out."

CHAPTER 10 | John

"Do your bit by growing a bit of something."
—The Note Book, *Port Arthur Daily News*,
1915

My sister ain't going to drag me there, especially not after trying to drown me. I swung my arm around hard. Saara let go. She stomped off on her way to Mrs. Entwhistle's house. I followed her at my own speed.

Raindrops splattered the dusty back lane. Saara glanced back at me with her hands on her hips, so I decided to race her. At our neighbour's house, we jostled each other up the back stairs. Mrs. Entwhistle must have seen us or heard us 'cause the door opened when we reached the top step.

"Hello, Saara, John," she said, waving us inside.

Yum. Her kitchen smelled of cinnamon. She opened her cookie jar and set it on the table, saying, "Help yourselves to a snickerdoodle and have a seat." We did as we was told. She lowered herself onto the wooden chair. "I have a proposition for you two."

"Is that a grammar lesson?" I asked, licking cinnamon sugar off my lips. "I get enough of them from my sister."

Saara giggled. I glared her way. I wasn't trying to be funny.

"No, young man," said Mrs. Entwhistle. "It is a scheme that will help all of us. You see, right before Mr. Entwhistle joined the Fifty-Second Battalion, he dug up our backyard and planted the garden. But"—she patted her bulging front—"with growing my baby so well, I simply cannot manage the weeding. If you strong young people will care for the garden, our households can share the vegetables. I'm not even certain of everything my husband planted."

I frowned. Working in a garden was pure drudgering. This spring, Mama wanted to start a garden of our own. It would save us money, she said. Our backyard was too shaded. So she got me to fill out the form to get permission to grow vegetables on the vacant lot on Foley Street. We got the permit, but we ran out of time to start planting. I thought I got off scot-free.

Botheration! Saara was saying, "Of course we can do that, Mrs. Entwhistle."

I clamped my mouth shut so I didn't groan out loud.

"That's wonderful," said Mrs. Entwhistle. "I knew you two were the right ones to ask."

Trying to stop frowning, I said, "We can't do any work till the rain shower's over."

"Well, then, have some more snickerdoodles."

My frown disappeared as I reached in and came up with three cookies. Saara took only one.

Mrs. Entwhistle chuckled at her, saying, "You don't have to be so polite, dear," and handed her another cookie. "Now, you'll find the gardening tools in the shed, and the buckets are next to the rain barrel." As we headed out the door, she called after us, "Thank you."

Saara made a beeline home because of the rain. *Sissy sister.* I liked feeling the drops splash my face.

On my way to find Fred, I thought about Mr. Serious *again*. For the hundredth time, at least. With the German spies confessing, I wondered if Mr. Serious was a spy, too. *What was he up to yesterday?*

Later, there I was, shooting marbles with Fred beside our house, when I heard that awful Bossy Sister voice.

"The rain's stopped. It's time to attack the garden plot," ordered Saara.

"Aw—I'm winning and I hardly ever beat Fred," I grumbled. "Can't we wait until tomorrow?"

She grabbed my arm, saying, "No, we can't." She started dragging me away.

"Let go!" I shouted and yanked my arm free. "I'm still mad at you for trying to drown me."

"Look, I'm sorry I held you under—I had to do *something* to get your attention."

"Don't *ever* do that again."

We stepped into the back lane. I snatched a handful of dirt and pebbles and hurled it at a tree trunk. "Dumb garden."

Saara took a deep breath. "Think about all the people we're helping."

All I did was grunt.

"Remember how much Mama wanted to plant a garden this year?"

"Yeah," I grumped. I knew this chore was the right thing to do. It even helped the war effort. I just didn't like working in a garden, and I didn't want to be bossed around.

"This will save our family money."

I might as well agree with her 'cause she ain't going to quit until I do. "Yeah, okay," I mumbled. I shuffled toward the Entwhistles' backyard. "At least we don't have to haul any water today, thanks to the rain."

Saara found a hoe in the shed and handed it to me. "Drat," she said, "there's only one. Next time we'll bring ours."

My sister bent down to look at the plants. "Thank goodness I learned a few things from Aunt Marja. We need to find the rows Mr. Entwhistle planted. Then you can hoe between them and I'll pull the weeds in the rows." Digging her heel in the earth, she marked the ends of the first two rows. She pointed to the space in between and said, "Start here."

"Yeah, boss." I hacked at the greenery.

Much later, I said, "Can I go play with Fred now?"

"We've worked for barely ten minutes! Stop your whinging." She sounded upset.

I was sure we'd been at this for at least thirty minutes already.

"Look," said Saara, "how about we get half the weeding done today?"

I worked hard and finished two whole rows. Time for a drink. I scooped a handful of water from the rain barrel, then leaned on my hoe.

Saara heaved a sigh. It felt like she was scolding me. What was so wrong with taking a little rest?

"I know what'll help us keep weeding," said Saara. "Let's play Miss Rodgers's favourite game—Twenty Questions."

"One round, that's all," I said.

"I'm thinking of a place."

"This stupid garden?" I griped.

"No, silly. That would be too easy. Ask again."

"Our house?"

"No."

"Fred's house?"

"No."

I named several more buildings as I hoed more weeds. No, no, no. Finally I asked, "Is it even in Port Arthur?"

Saara grinned and said, "No."

"Is it a city?"

"Yes."

I guessed every city I could think of, except the one she had in mind. I whacked the dirt with the hoe. "Why'd you make it so hard? Is it even in Ontario?"

Saara hauled out a stubborn long-rooted weed and said, "No."

"Quebec?"

"Yes."

"Yes, Quebec the city, or yes, Quebec the province?"

"No and yes—you have two questions left."

"Montreal, it has to be Montreal. Is it Montreal?"

"You got it."

I threw down the hoe and plucked a wide blade of grass. Pressing it to my lips, I blew a piercing screech to celebrate. "Okay, I have a person."

"I'm not guessing until you're hoeing again." Saara

waited until I started where I'd left off. "Is the person male?"

"Yes."

After more questions to narrow down who it was, she asked, "Is he Canadian?"

"No."

She named several non-Canadians we knew. No, no, no.

"Only one more guess, Saara. Bet you can't get it," I taunted.

She breathed deep. "Kaiser Wilhelm?"

"NO! He is German, though. Come on, Saara. I'll let you have one more question."

"Tell me who it is."

"Carl Schmidt—you know, one of the German spies who just confessed."

Her whole face blushed as she nodded. She remembered him now. "Only one more row and we can stop for today."

"Sure, boss," I said, grinning. After we was done and home, I was still laughing over beating my sister.

CHAPTER 11 | Saara

"Germany's submarine triumphs will come to an end one of these days, when Norway runs out of merchant ships."—The Note Book, *Port Arthur Daily News*, 1915

Helena slipped into the church pew beside me with a tiny wave of her hand. She kept her head down while saying hello. She was wearing her mother's wide-brimmed Sunday hat. I could see part of her face, and it looked fine to me—just a few faint blemishes. She stared at her hands all through the service. As soon as the pastor finished the announcements, she darted outside. Was she upset over what I'd said about the wax? It hurt to think we might not be friends anymore over something so petty.

John and I returned to the Entwhistles' garden on Monday for our third stint of weeding. We finished clearing the garden of weeds. I had to dig deep in my bag of tricks to keep John working. He was so lazy!

Back at home, I finally figured out the ladder mathematics problem, but now the next one had me stumped. *What is the weight of a cast-iron block 6 inches long, 5 inches wide, and 3 inches high? The block is a rectangular parallelepiped and weighs .26 pounds per cubic inch.* I panicked. My brain hurt. Richard would know how to solve it. But if I asked him for help, the teasing he'd give me would hurt worse.

There were only ten days left to get everything done. I'd forgotten to record the temperature after supper the last two nights. Once because Mama needed help making strawberry jam, and last night it was John's fault. He'd fallen in a mucky puddle, so Mama made *me* scrub his knickers and shirt. From now on I had to remember to check the thermometer *every* evening. My graph had the wrong dates, so I changed them.

I wiped my sweaty palms on my dress, then refilled my teacup. I would finish all of this work no matter what. I faced the problem about weight again.

A breeze swooped in through the open kitchen window and ruffled my papers. John's commands drifted in from outdoors. "Me and Fred're on the French ship. You be the German submarine hunting us."

"I don't want to shoot you," said a voice I didn't recognize. I peeked around the curtain. The voice belonged to an unfamiliar blond boy slightly taller than John.

"That's okay, Peter," said Fred, "we'll do the firing and sink you." He and John raised their stick rifles and cheered, too preoccupied to notice Peter's frown.

Was Peter part of the family that had just moved into the house next to Fred's? Leaning over the sink, I called out the window, "Why don't you play explorers and work together?"

"That's boring," yelled John.

I said, "Then John, you be the German spy trying to blow up a bridge and Fred and Peter can arrest you and take you to the internment—" Now Fred was frowning. *Oh!* What a dumb thing for me to say.

"Keep your nose out of this, Saara. We want a battle," said John. "Come on, fellas, let's go somewheres else."

I settled back to my school work. I had finally remembered the formula for volume and was making progress.

On my last gulp of tea, John stormed into the house to find me. "Why'd you have to ruin everything?" he said. "We was doing fine until you butted in. Now Peter's run off saying he won't play with us anymore."

"What did you do to him?"

"Nothing! We was just playing. We finished sinking him, then Fred was Russia and I was England an' we attacked him from front and back ..." John blathered on and on *and on*, recounting every detail of their skirmish. It was hard to keep paying attention.

He stopped at the sound of someone knocking on our door. "Maybe Peter changed his mind," said John hopefully. I followed him down the hall and through the porch.

Out front stood a girl who looked about my age, her two braids almost as blond as mine. She was holding Sipu and stroking her head. My cat purred loudly in response. The girl handed Sipu to me, saying, "You have a beautiful cat." Turning toward my brother, she asked, "Are you John?" He nodded. "I am Birgitta. I am the sister of Peter."

"I'm John's sister, Saara," I said. "He told me Peter's upset. What's wrong?"

"That is why I came," said Birgitta. "He was picked on all this past year in Toronto. When we moved here, we thought it would be better."

"Why was he picked on?" asked John.

"For being German. Our family name is Schmidt."

John's eyes saucered. "Are you relatives of Carl Schmidt, the spy? I've been reading about him in the papers."

I shushed John.

"No," said Birgitta. "*Schmidt* is like the English name *Smith*. Many, many families. The police asked my father the same question." She sighed. "I hoped it would be different for Peter here."

"Who's been picking on him here?" I asked. Instantly I understood, and I turned around so sharply Sipu jumped out of my arms. Glaring at John, I said, "How could you treat a new friend like that?"

"It wasn't on purpose. We didn't know he was German, honest. But in our war games he always ended up being the Hun."

"John!" I cringed at him saying *Hun* in front of Birgitta. It likened Germans to barbarians.

"Sorry, Birgitta," he backpedalled, "I mean, the German."

"I am used to it," said Birgitta with a shrug. Sipu curled around her legs in a figure eight.

"I'll go 'pologize," said John as he hurried away to find Peter.

"Your brother is awfully kind," said Birgitta.

"It's strange. Usually he's simply awful."

Birgitta stared at me for a moment, and then she laughed. She said something in German, then switched back to English. "Little brothers are like ... like ..." She plucked the tip of a tall grass stalk and pretended it was stuck to her sock. "Like this," she said.

"Exactly!" I exclaimed. "They're like prickly burrs!"

Birgitta bent to pat Sipu. My cat lay on her side, inviting Birgitta to rub her stomach. I liked Birgitta's view of brothers and her kindly way with Sipu. "Come inside and have a cardamom cookie," I said, leading the way to the kitchen.

After our sweet snack, Birgitta said with pride, "Now come to my house. I want to show you my German bisque dolls."

I wasn't fond of dolls but welcomed her friendly invitation. I hadn't realized how lonely I was feeling. My summer was looking up.

CHAPTER 12 | John

"Your country needs you."—The Note Book, *Port Arthur Daily News,* 1915

I was awake before my Big Ben rang Wednesday morning. Like every day for the past week, my first thought was of Mr. Serious being up to no good. The way he kept to himself. How he cradled his knapsack instead of wearing it on his back.

I sat up in bed with a start as I remembered something. Last night, when Peter and I had been playing outside his house, his father and I had bumped into each other by accident and he said, "*Verzeihung.*" It was the same word Mr. Serious'd said to me. Mr. Serious *was* German! I *had* to tell the police. Would they believe me? Not likely. But maybe they'd believe someone else. Someone they already trusted. I knew the perfect man. If only I could convince him.

After I unset the alarm, I rushed to dress and took off to meet Fred. I tapped on his front door. It took him a few minutes to come out.

"Say, Fred, remember the guy with the knapsack on the streetcar on Dominion Day?"

"What guy?"

"You know, the one who tripped over my feet?"

"Okay. I sort of remember."

"I think he's a sabotager."

"What? Quit pulling my leg."

"I ain't joking. Let's go. I want to tell Cam."

At the *Daily News* building, there was no sign of Cam or his motorcar.

Fred pulled a handful of marbles from his knickers pocket, saying, "Want to play?"

I shook my head.

In a few minutes, some other guys arrived and Fred got his game.

Later, when Joe started heaving out the stacks of papers, I ran to help.

"Morning, Joe," I said. "Do you know when Cam, uh, I mean, Mr. Cameron will show up?"

"He should be along soon."

Fred grabbed a sheaf of papers. "You coming, Johnny?"

"Not yet. Go on ahead."

"Okay if I take your corner?"

"Sure. If you'll do my paper route, too."

"Bully!" he said, flashing a monster grin.

I fished a crumpled paper out of my knickers pocket and spread it open. The ink was still readable. I handed the list to Fred. "Here's all the addresses."

"Thanks."

"Watch out for the mean dog on Sheppard Street."

All the newsboys was long gone when Cam finally drove up. Before he even got the motor turned off, I was blurting my story. I told him every detail I could remember about Mr. Serious.

"And last Wednesday, I found some evidence up by the wireless station," I said, showing him the bullet casing.

He used my handkerchief to carefully lift the cylinder and turn it around. After examining it closely, he said, "It's definitely not from a police gun. Might be from the saboteur's. Good thing you didn't get your fingerprints on it. You should turn this in to the police."

"Sure." I tucked the little bundle back in my pocket. "Are you gonna tell them about Mr. Serious?"

"I want to know more about his knapsack."

"He was real careful with it. Kept it on his lap. Then he carried it in his arms, close like, instead of on his back. Looked as if he didn't want it bumped."

"You think he had dynamite in there?"

"Maybe. I don't know—I just know what I seen."

"Hmm ... it does sound suspicious." He removed his cap and scratched the back of his head. "Okay, I'll go see Constable Bryant."

"Can I come with you, Cam? Please?"

"What did I tell you last time you asked that?"

"You said, 'I report, you sell the papers.' But I'm too late now to hawk papers, and Fred's doing my route for me."

"Well, Johnny, seeing as you gave me the scoop here, all right. But keep your mouth shut."

I climbed into the passenger seat. My first real scouting for the facts with a reporter! Cam grabbed the steering wheel and we roared off to the police station. Dust billowed from under the tires.

Before long, Cam pulled up and parked. He held his finger to his lips, then said, "I'll do the talking."

Once inside, Cam asked for Constable Bryant.

The police officer appeared a few minutes later. "Hello, Cam, what's news?" he said, stretching out his hand in greeting.

Cam shook it and pointed to me. "My pal Johnny, here, has something to show you."

I retrieved the wrapped bullet casing and placed the bundle in the constable's palm. "He tells me he found it near the wireless station the day after saboteurs struck."

Constable Bryant unwrapped and inspected the casing. He nodded, saying, "Good work, lad."

"Johnny also saw a suspicious man with a knapsack near Current River Park on Dominion Day."

"Oh?" said the police officer, his eyebrows raised. "What was suspicious about him, Johnny?"

I questioned Cam with my eyes: *Can I speak?*

Cam said, "Go ahead—just the facts."

I repeated everything I'd told Cam. Then I remembered what the man had said. "When he tripped over my feet he said something foreign that could have been German."

"How do you know German?" asked the constable.

"I learned a few words from my new friend Peter Schmidt, and I heard his father say some."

Cam pressed his hand on my shoulder. I think he was telling me to shut my mouth again. Cam said, "What do you think, Constable? Is it time to inspect the railway bridge?"

"Yes, I'd say that's called for. Let me guess—you want to be there?" he said with a sly smile.

"You know I do," replied Cam.

"Then let's get it done." He handed the casing back to me. That was peculiar. Didn't the police want to keep it? I knew I did, so there was no argument from me.

Constable Bryant rounded up a couple of other officers. Me and Cam trailed their police cars out to the bridge. With all the bushes growing on the banks, I could hardly see Current River.

When I stepped out of Cam's motorcar, my knees was shaky. What would the police find?

"Sorry, Johnny," said Cam, "this is as far as you go. If there's dynamite, it could blow sky-high." He took off after the policemen.

Rats. I'm so close! I balanced on my toes on the running board to get a better view. The men searched this side of the bridge. They sure was taking their time.

"Bryant! Over here!" shouted one of the officers from near a bridge support.

Everyone rushed over to him.

A few minutes passed, then Cam raised his arm and signalled for me to come, too.

Before he could change his mind, I sprinted to the spot. The men was staring down a hole as an officer cleared more dirt. Inside was several sticks of dynamite! Right in front of my eyes!

"Aren't we in danger, Cam?" I whispered.

"Nope—the blasting caps are missing," he said. "The guy must be planning to come back."

"But he won't find his cache," said Constable Bryant. "Well done, Johnny," he said, shaking my hand so hard my ribs rattled.

"Come on, pal," said Cam, messing my hair. "I've got an Extra to write for you to sell." We dashed to his car and sped back to the *Daily News*.

Cam ran inside to get his report done. An Extra was mighty special. They only came out when there was news so important it couldn't wait till morning. I couldn't believe this one was all because of me! Every five minutes I waited, I felt a all-new thrill.

When Cam reappeared, he said, "It shouldn't take much longer."

"Thanks heaps for letting me go along today, Cam."

"You deserved it. From now on, I'm calling you Scoop."

I grinned from ear to ear.

"Bye, Scoop," hollered Cam as he drove off. That grin didn't leave my face until Cam was long gone.

Finally the Extra edition was ready. I was the first newsboy to get my copies. I didn't have to go to my usual corner—an Extra meant it was every boy for himself. Sell anywhere and everywhere. I had the jump on the other fellows and wanted to sell as many papers as I could before they found out.

I ran to Cumberland Street and shouted, "EXTRA! EXTRA! Read all about it! *SABOTAGE THWARTED! DYNAMITE FOUND RIGHT HERE IN PORT ARTHUR!*" People swarmed me, anxious to buy Cam's report.

I'd read it quick and I was surprised by all of the "extra" information. The way he wrote the story, you'd think the very next train to cross the river would have set off a gigantic explosion, wrecking the bridge and the entire train, killing everyone on board. It was bully!

"A German-Canadian from Berlin, Ontario, has
given his life for the British Empire on the fields
of France, and a German-Canadian has written to
General Hughes offering his services. There are many
more German-Canadians who would take up arms
against their birthplace, not that they love Germany
less perhaps, but that they love freedom more."
—The Note Book, *Port Arthur Daily News*, 1915

After lunch on Saturday, I headed to Birgitta's house.
Yesterday I could tell I was needing a break from homework, so I'd invited her to go with me today to the Red
Cross garden party—no boys allowed. At least, not our
brothers, especially John.

When Birgitta answered my knock on her door, the
most mouth-watering aroma wafted out of the house.
"Hi, Saara. Mutti baked strudel. Come and join us."

"Thank you. I've never had strudel, but my nose tells
me it's going to taste wonderful." I followed Birgitta
inside. I'd already met everyone except her father.

"Vati, this is my friend Saara," said Birgitta. To me
she whispered, "*Vati* means 'father.'"

"*Guten tag*, Saara, hello," said Mr. Schmidt.

"Hello," I answered.

Birgitta's parents, her little sister, and Peter were crowded around their small kitchen table. Still they made room for one more. Mutti cut a slice of strudel and handed it to me.

"Thank you very much." I took a bite. The flaky pastry with apple filling tasted heavenly. "This is delicious."

Mr. Schmidt didn't say much, but he smiled a lot. When Birgitta offered me a second piece of strudel, I said, "No, thank you." I wanted to have room for treats at the garden party.

We excused ourselves and set off down the hill to Algoma Street. Our long loose hair blew out behind us. We'd decided to skip our usual braids for the party.

"I translated some of the newspaper for my father," said Birgitta, her face clouded with concern.

Was it John's scoop about the dynamite and German saboteur? That news would cause them concern. "What part?" I asked.

"It was about the city leaders, and it scared me."

"What did it say?"

"They are very worried after what happened at the railway bridge that enemy aliens will damage grain elevators and other important buildings. So worried they want to send even more enemy aliens away to internment camps. Already every German family we know here has had their business and home searched for weapons. The police asked Vati again why he moved here from Toronto. They do not seem to believe it was for better work."

All I could think to say was "Perhaps the war will end before they intern any more people."

We walked on in silence, passing the streetcar stop.

"We are not taking the streetcar?" asked Birgitta.

"It's a long walk, but if we don't have to use our coins for streetcar fare, we should have enough for ice cream."

"That is fine with me," said Birgitta with a smile.

Traffic became heavier once we reached Court Street. As the sky darkened, I prayed the rain would hold off. Snatches of military music reached our ears. At the entrance to an estate stood a large white screen with a huge Red Cross emblem. We joined the crowd flocking onto the property.

"The Red Cross is always looking for more volunteers to knit socks," I said. "I've seen the socks you make— they actually have heels."

But Birgitta wasn't listening. "Oh, Saara, look at the lights and beautiful flowers. *Ein märchenland* ... a fairytale land." Strings of twinkling coloured electric lights stretched from tree to tree behind the festive tables on the lawn. Chinese lanterns hung from the branches. Union Jacks and flags of the Allied countries decorated the verandas of the mansion. Lined up in front of the house was booth after booth, selling everything from buttermilk to vegetables to home baking to bouquets of pale pink and deep red peonies.

"There's the ice cream booth," I said. "Come on."

We plunked our coins on the table and drooled as our dishes were heaped with strawberry ice cream and first-of-the-season Dorion strawberries. Their scent was entrancing.

"Thank you," we said in unison, then carried our treats to the edge of the lawn. From where we sat cross-legged on the grass, we could see the high-stepping Scottish dancers. Every so often the thwack of a racket hitting the ball drifted over to us from the tennis court.

Two girls wearing white blouses, colourful skirts, and head scarves, as well as several strands of beads, guided visitors to tents at the back of the yard. What were these "gypsy" girls up to? After we scraped (and licked) our dishes clean and returned them, we decided to find out. The gypsy girls approached people all around us but avoided Birgitta and me.

When I tapped the blonde gypsy on the shoulder, she spun around, eyed us, and said, "I can only take you to the palmist if you're wearing a patriotic button."

Birgitta asked, "What is a palmist?"

"Fortune teller," the girl said.

I grimaced, remembering the last time I'd had my future predicted and it came true more terribly than I'd ever imagined. Black spots had formed on the "boat" when Uncle Arvo dropped the New Year's molten lead in cold water. That little sign of sadness foretold a horrific shipwreck that claimed over a thousand lives.

"I'm not interested," I said. "But you can do it if you want."

"I want to," said Birgitta. "Where do I get a button?"

The gypsy pointed to a booth in the centre. "It costs ten cents."

Birgitta's face crumpled in disappointment. I knew we each had only a nickel left. If I gave Birgitta mine, I'd have nothing left for candy. Hoping for a good prediction for her, I handed her my coin. "Here, you can have this."

"Thank you, Saara. You are a true friend."

With a button pinned to her dress and a grin lighting up her face, Birgitta trailed the gypsy girl to learn her fate. At the door of the tent, I hung back. Birgitta motioned me forward. "You can come in with me. You have a share in this fortune."

I wasn't sure I liked the sound of that, but I followed her inside. By the dim light of a lantern we took our seats at a small table. Across from us sat a tiny woman wearing even more beads and colours than the gypsy girls. She reached for my right hand. I withdrew it quickly, saying, "It's for my friend—here" as I pushed Birgitta's hand toward her.

The fortune teller took her hand, and her brow furrowed slightly. Then her golden hooped earrings glinted as she tilted her head, studying Birgitta's palm. She mumbled "hmm" and "a-ha" and "yes," then "hmm" again. Finally she said, "You have a loving family. A strong family. This is good. You have a long journey ahead—"

"To where?" asked Birgitta.

"I cannot tell."

"Will the war end soon so I can visit my cousins?"

"Where do your cousins live?"

"In Germany."

The woman dropped Birgitta's hand as if it were a hot

potato. "There is no happiness," she snapped. She ripped the patriotic button off Birgitta's dress, tearing the fabric. "Now go. Germans are not welcome here."

Speechless, we scrambled out of the tent and collided with the gypsy girl. She must have been eavesdropping. "You've really upset my mother. You must leave the property."

Birgitta said bravely, "I do not want the war any more than you do. But I will go." She said nothing else until we were a block away, then blurted, "People are so unfair. I was born in Germany but it does not mean ..." She wept.

I put my arm around her shoulders, saying, "I know."

After a few moments she mopped her face with her handkerchief. "I think the fortune teller was a fake. I do not believe what she said about a journey."

On our walk home, Birgitta talked about everything but the palmist. She spent a few minutes patting each cat along the way, including Tiger in front of Mr. Campbell's house. The sun broke through the clouds, raising the temperature and our spirits. Birgitta left me, waving cheerfully.

It was Sunday morning and we were waiting for the pastor to begin the service. My head was swimming with pronouns, participles, and parsing of verbs. I'd finished all of my grammar work, two compositions, and the rough copy of my essay. Under my breath I said, "Whew." Four more days to get my essay, last composition, and the rest of my mathematics done.

To my surprise, Helena joined me in the pew. "Helena! I haven't seen you in so long—"

"Who's the new girl?" she whispered in my ear. She must have seen me and Birgitta walking past her house.

"Her name's Birgitta Schmidt. She's—" was all I could get out before Mama shushed me. Helena gave me a puzzled, almost angry look. She didn't sing any of the hymns. The pastor preached his sermon, but I hardly paid attention, trying to figure out what was bothering Helena.

"In conclusion, pay heed to these words of our Lord," said the pastor, bringing my focus back to his sermon. "The text is from the book of Matthew, chapter five, verse forty-four. 'But I say unto you, Love your enemies, bless them that curse you, do good to them that hate you, and pray for them which despitefully use you, and persecute you.'"

As soon as the service ended, Helena grabbed my arm and steered me outside. "How can you possibly associate with a Hun? The Germans murdered Gordon! Their submarines blow up Allied steamships!"

"Birgitta doesn't agree with the war. She's from a good family—"

"What are they hiding? Her father could be plotting to destroy our country."

"How can you say such things when you haven't even met her?" My voice sounded harsher than I'd intended.

With an ugly glare, Helena said, "Stay away from her and all of the enemy aliens." She spun on her heel and strode toward home, clearly not wanting my company. I guessed she hadn't heard any of the sermon.

How dare she order me around! It was none of her business who my friends were. Right now, Birgitta was more of a friend to me than Helena had time—or wanted—to be. Besides, I had more urgent things to focus on. The deadline for my assignments was coming fast.

CHAPTER 14 | John

"An eastern hen has laid an eight-inch egg, but until it explodes it will gain little publicity on the pages now devoted to war news."—The Note Book, *Port Arthur Daily News*, 1915

Cam drove into the lane ahead of me and Fred on Monday morning and hopped out of his motorcar. I ran to catch him before he was beyond reach inside the *Daily News* building.

"Wait, Cam," I called. "I gotta ask you something."

"Okay, Scoop, but make it snappy."

"That Extra you wrote about the dynamite—how come you reported that the dynamite sticks could've exploded at any time? That's not what the police said. There was no blasting caps, so no danger, right?"

"Right."

"Aren't you supposed to report the facts?"

"So I embellished the facts a little. We're in the business of selling newspapers, right?"

"Sure, but—"

"Did you have any trouble selling the Extra edition?" he said, reaching for the door handle.

"No, sir. Sold the most ever."

"Okay, then. Relax, Scoop," he said. "Mission accomplished." With that he opened the door and disappeared inside. The roar of the presses blasted my ears. As much as I wanted to deny it, Saara was right. Not all reports was true and real.

"Quiet, fellas," I said. "Saara's prob'ly still working in the garden." Me and Fred and Peter sneaked along the back lane and hid behind the Entwhistles' shed. We was hunting with my camera.

Me and Saara had agreed that she'd work on half the garden alone this morning ("in peace," she'd said), and I would weed the other half this afternoon ("And then I can finish the good copy of my essay," she'd said). *That girl is far too serious. All she can think about is homework.*

I signalled Peter and Fred to keep shushed. Then I peeked around the corner. Yup, she was there. She was facing the other way, bent over double.

Click.

At the sound of my camera, Saara stood straight with weeds in her hands. Before she could turn and spot me, I slipped behind the shed. Us boys tried to smother our chuckling. Then I snorted.

"John, what are you up to now?" called Saara.

How did she know it was me? I peered around the shed and held up my camera. "Oh, just taking pictures of scenery in the neighbourhood to send to the wounded soldiers."

"Then why in the world did you take a picture of my backside?"

"I may need to mail that one to a future soldier in North Branch," I said, snickering.

"You wouldn't dare send it to Mikko!" she yelled, throwing the weeds at me, but they fell short.

How come she can't ever take a joke?

CHAPTER 15 | Saara

"The school promotion examination lists are published in today's Daily News. Takes us back to the times when we played hookey, and truant officers were unheard of."—The Note Book, *Port Arthur Daily News*, 1915

I jumped up from writing my composition and darted to the kitchen window. It was eight-thirty in the evening and I'd forgotten to get the last temperature! Right now it was 79 degrees Fahrenheit. At six o'clock it must have been a couple of degrees warmer, say 81. It would have to do—tomorrow was the due date. I entered *81* to complete my graph.

Now, one more page to go in this composition and I'd be done all of my homework! I reread the assignment to gather my thoughts.

Discuss this quote from Lord Dufferin:
Love your country, believe in her, honour her, work for her, live for her, die for her. Never has any people been endowed with a nobler birthright or blessed with prospects of a fairer future.

Come on, tired brain—think! Hunched over, I set my pencil in motion. I forced myself to keep at it until the page was full. Then I corrected the whole composition and copied it into my scribbler.

"There. All finished." I yawned. Everyone else had gone to bed ages ago. After checking and rechecking my two long weeks of hard work, I closed my scribbler. As I turned off the kitchen light, I felt grateful that we had gotten electricity in our neighbourhood the year before, so I didn't have to do my work by the dim light of a candle. It still seemed like a bit of a miracle.

Come morning, I quickly dressed and charged down to the kitchen. I planned to see Mr. Graham at nine o'clock sharp and hand him my scribbler. Mama and John were already eating breakfast.

"I'll eat after I get back," I said. Sliding my homework sheets and textbooks aside, I gasped. "Where's my scribbler? I left it right here on the table!"

"Are you sure you didn't take it up to your bedroom last night?" asked Mama, sipping her coffee.

"No, I—" My brother's smirk caught my eye. "John, what did you do with it? This isn't funny."

His face turned angelic. "I didn't touch it. Honest."

"Then why were you smirking?"

"I was just thinking about my name being in the school promotion list in today's paper and yours ain't."

I flinched. I'd forgotten about that list. Would anyone besides my brother notice my name missing? "John, you were up early. You must have seen my scribbler and hidden it. How could you do something so mean? I HATE you!"

"Saara! That's uncalled for," said Mama, frowning. "Jussi, you wouldn't hide her notebook, would you?"

"No, Mama. I never saw it." John glared at me, then drained his glass. He plunked it next to the sink and took off outdoors.

"Then where could it be?" Feeling ill with dread, I scoured the kitchen and parlour, searching for my scribbler. There was no sign of it. Perhaps sensing my distress, Sipu was yowling, so I let her out. *God, please help me find my homework.*

If it was upstairs, *I* certainly didn't put it there. But I had to check everywhere. I started in the most likely spot: my brother's bedroom. John had sounded sincere, but I didn't believe him. It was exactly like him to pull a hurtful prank on me. I opened his top dresser drawer and rooted around. Only underwear and socks. The next drawer held shirts and a pair of knickers. One drawer left. I slid it open.

Aha! There was my scribbler in plain view! What a bold liar.

He needed to be taught a lesson: a prank for a prank. I would steal something precious to him. Before I could change my mind, I grabbed his budget and scrapbook of newspaper clippings from the top of the dresser. I carried them to my bedroom and shoved them under my mattress. My conscience objected, saying, "Don't be childish," but I ignored it.

Then a black smudge on the back of my scribbler caught my eye. Not only had my brother stolen it, but he'd made a mess of it as well. *Arrrg!* What damage had he done to my work inside? I opened it and stared in horror. It wasn't my handwriting—it was John's! I flipped through the scribbler. Page after page was full of his practice newspaper articles, signed "John Mäki, Cub Reporter, *Port Arthur Daily News.*" There was his report on the arrest of Carl Schmidt and Gustav Stephen in March, then one about Alien Day on April 3, when all enemy aliens had to report to the police station on Cooke Street. His last article was called *THE WAR EFFORT: EVERYONE DO YOUR PART: MEN OLD ENOUGH, GO FIGHT, WOMEN SEW, KNIT, SCRIMP, GROW VEGETABLES!* He definitely needed to work on shortening his headlines to save some facts for his articles.

I put his scribbler back where I'd found it, and a sob welled up in my throat. I choked it down. I was back where I started: my scribbler was still missing. Half-heartedly, I searched my bedroom again. Mama assured me she'd thoroughly checked her and Papa's bedroom and her sewing area in the corner.

After washing the breakfast dishes, I was at a loss as to what more I could do to find my scribbler. But I couldn't give up. Maybe if I took a break to read for a while, it would turn up when I searched the house again. It was already getting hot indoors, so I grabbed a book and stretched out on the cool grass in the shade to read.

I woke up in a flap—a flap of wings. Chicken wings to be precise. And John's fit of laughter. "Get out of here," I said, shooing him and the bird away.

He stepped back, holding the chicken by its feet. It squawked and twisted and flapped. John said, "I know you was mad that I spent my money on a camera and this old farmer stopped me this morning sayin', 'Sonny, you want a gold mine and help the war effort?' I figured you'd be happy if I brought home a hen so Mama doesn't have to pay for eggs anymore."

I scowled.

"How come you ain't happy about this?" he asked, as sincere as could be.

"*Aren't. Aren't* happy. I aren't happy because—*ooooob*. Now I can't even talk properly."

"It's okay."

"No, nothing's okay! When I find my scribbler, then I'll be happy. You *have* to tell me where you hid it."

"But I don't know anything about it," he insisted. Then he mumbled, "Well, I bet Mama'll think the chicken is a good idea."

"Wait. Let's think this through. First, how do you know that hen can actually lay an egg? It looks close to dying."

He stared at the bird.

"If it *can* lay an egg, who's going to pay for chicken feed?"

John opened his mouth to answer, but I cut him off. "And where are you going to keep it? Your bedroom is such a mess you'd hardly notice the bird in there, but we'd smell it all through the house."

My brother skulked away.

"Besides, Mama would never let you keep it inside."

"Fine," he mumbled, sounding hurt. "I guess Mama

can stew the hen." John disappeared around the corner of the house. His voice still reached me, saying, "I'll leave the newspaper open on the table for you. The 'Letter from the Front' is from your pal Elias."

I brushed off my dress and headed inside. John stuffed the chicken in a lidded basket and then climbed the stairs to tell Mama.

Elias used to work at the Star Livery, until he left for England in February to drive an ambulance car. On page two, I read:

Dear friends in Port Arthur,
Many thanks for the comfort box you sent me through the Red Cross (methinks a certain Miss Sarah had a role?).
I am feeling fine and dandy at present and busy with transporting the wounded here in France.
You can feel right proud of our Canadian boys. They hold up bravely in the fight, with shells bursting all about. I have nothing against the soldiers, but I hate their trade. The slaughter of soldiers—and horses, too—makes me sick. I can only hope that the world will soon be so sick of the horrors of war that the nation that tries to begin another one will be an outcast of the human race.
Please don't send me any more tobacco or sox or anything at all. We get plenty of everything here. Just send plenty of letters. That is what I want, news about home.

Elias included his address, care of the British Expeditionary Force. How could I write to him without telling him about our favourite stable horse, Chief, being sent to France? It would break his heart. I hated to admit that the best thing to send would be John's budget full of news.

I made a sandwich to take outside with my book. Later, when I looked at the clock, it was already two o'clock. I turned the house inside out again. Nothing. The afternoon crept forward, feeling like three days. I kept hunting until the last minute, hoping my scribbler would reappear. Finally, I had to accept my sickening defeat and go face Mr. Graham.

When I reached his office, he was tidying the few remaining papers on his desk.

"Ah, Miss Mäki," he said, "you're cutting it close. I was about to leave."

When I set the textbooks on his desk, he asked, "Where is your work?"

"I completed *everything*, sir," I said, "but overnight it went missing." My voice was shaking.

He frowned. "Our agreement was that you would deliver your work on or before today."

"I know, sir, and I've searched from floor to ceiling at home—"

"If you *truly* intend to become a teacher, Miss Mäki, this work is critical. I will return here briefly in the morning. You have until quarter past eight to produce your assignments." He tucked the papers in his desk, stood, and donned his bowler hat. "Good day."

I *had* to find my scribbler.

Back at home, Mama was plucking the bird. When I told her my new deadline, she promised to ask Papa when he came home if he'd seen my scribbler. He was going to be working late, and then he'd attend a labour meeting. Meanwhile, I combed every square inch of our house between chores.

After our tough-old-hen supper, Mama settled in to mend a pair of Papa's trousers while I scrubbed the dishes. John clipped articles from today's newspaper, then headed upstairs to fetch his scrapbook and budget. I held my breath—he was about to feel the shock of his own belongings going missing. That would teach him. He clomped around the painted floor of his bedroom for several seconds. Then he hurtled down the steps back to the kitchen.

"Mama, did you clean my room?" he asked.

"No. I haven't been in there for days."

"Saara, what did you do with my scrapbook?"

"Why would I want your stupid scrapbook?" I said.

"It's not stupid! And my budget's gone, too. Both of them were on top of my dresser this morning."

I shrugged. "You must have misplaced them."

"I was out all day except to bring the chicken home. Where'd you put them?" he pleaded, visibly upset.

"Saara," said Mama, giving me a hard look. "You were the only one home besides me."

There was no way out. "He'll get them back when he returns my scribbler."

"I TOLD YOU ALREADY I NEVER SAW IT!" yelled John.

"That's enough, Jussi," said Mama in a firm voice. "Saara, give them back right now. Here I thought you were beyond such immature behaviour."

I'd thought so, too, but desperation brought out the worst in me. After drying my hands, I retrieved John's things and dumped them on the table. "I still don't believe you," I hissed.

I tried to wait up for Papa so I could run downstairs and ask him, but I must have fallen asleep. The slam of a door woke me with a jolt. My pulse throbbed from my temples to my toes. Papa's voice roared up through the heating pipes to my room until Mama shushed him. Only two words were clear: *union* and *fools*. This was *not* a good time to ask him.

The next morning, Mama shook her head and said, "I'm sorry, Saara. Papa was so worried about his job last night, I forgot to ask him about your notebook."

I wanted to burst into a tantrum like Baby Sanni.

Mama lifted the lid of the wood stove to kindle the fire. She grabbed a newspaper from the woodbox, and as she shook the top sheet loose, something fell out of the folds of paper. "Saara—I found your notebook!"

"How did I miss it yesterday?" I had sifted through that whole stack many times. "John sure hid it well."

"Now, Saara, you don't know—"

"Thank you, Mama," I said, cutting her off. "I need to deliver this." I brushed bits of moss and birch bark off my scribbler and fled toward the door. According to the parlour clock, I had just enough time to catch Mr. Graham. "I'll eat later." *Right after I wring my brother's neck.*

100

I bolted down the back lane, arms and legs pumping. I waved to Helena, who was pegging sheets on the clothesline. She saw me but didn't return my wave. Was she still upset over my new friendship with Birgitta? There was no time to stop. I kept running to the end of the back lane and for the whole two blocks along Secord Street, then turned at Cornwall.

Panting, I climbed the stairs into the school. The office was locked. The wall clock showed it was quarter past eight. I knocked loudly, but no one came to the door.

"Hello," called a man's voice from down the hall. Was it Mr. Graham? No, it was the custodian. "Do you need some help?"

I rushed over to him. "I have to find Principal Graham."

"He just said his farewells, miss."

"I need to get my schoolwork to him!"

"He's off home to collect his bags and catch the morning train. Come with me." The custodian strode to the office and unlocked the door. He jotted something on a scrap of paper and handed it to me. "Here's the address of the boarding house where he lives. You can try to catch him."

"Thank you," I said, grabbing the note and sprinting outside. *Please, God, give my feet wings.*

Several minutes later, I found the building. A horse and buggy stood out front, the driver in his seat, holding the reins. I knocked on the front door. A stout, ruddy-faced woman answered.

"Hello, ma'am. Is Mr. Graham here?"

Before she could speak, I had my answer as Mr. Graham careered down the stairway. "You're in the nick of time, Miss Mäki," he said, bumping his large suitcase on the banister.

"Here is my work, sir." I held out my scribbler.

"Slip it in my carpet bag, and make it quick," he said. "My driver will wait, but the train won't." I did so, and then he dashed to the street, flung his bags in the back of the buggy, and climbed up beside the driver. "Till September!" he bellowed as the driver urged the horse on.

Relief flooded me, and impulsively I hugged the woman. "Thank you, ma'am."

She blinked in surprise, then said, "Heaven's smiling on you today, girly."

By the time I got home, my relief had been replaced by fury. Rounding the corner of our porch, I spotted John and the other boys in front of Fred's house. John ran toward me, saying, "I heard you found your scribbler. Did you give it to Mr. Graham?" He sounded genuinely concerned. *What an actor.*

"I almost missed him because of *you*!"

"Saara, trust me. I never saw your scribbler yesterday."

"I don't trust you and I'll never trust you!" I said, pushing him aside and heading indoors.

Would Mr. Graham view my work as favourably as Miss Rodgers had? Doubt knotted deep within me. He was a stickler for correctness. I shuddered at the real and horrible possibility of having to repeat my year of school.

CHAPTER 16 | John

"If you can't fight you can at least help the Red Cross."
—The Note Book, *Port Arthur Daily News*, 1915

How could I ever make Saara believe it wasn't me who put her scribbler in the woodbox? Why did I even care? Maybe it was true what she said. That she would never, ever trust me. I kicked a stone clear across our lane.

When Saara'd come home from the farm, she was different. She'd grown up a whole bunch. She was more like Mama, so stuck on getting work done. Unbearable. I was trying all sorts of teasing and funny pranks to cheer her up and make her laugh. Nothing was working so far. But I wasn't ready to give up.

"Hey, John," called Fred. "We're waiting for you."

I trotted back to him and Peter. "So what did you decide to play?"

"Peter doesn't want to play war games this time," said Fred. "And I'm tired of cops and robbers."

Hearing him say "cops" reminded me of when they showed up to take his father away. "Have you heard from your father?"

"Yeah—we got one letter so far."

"What does he do at the internment camp?" Peter gasped. "Why was he sent there?"

"A whole bunch of Ukrainian men was rounded up at the end of June," I explained, so Fred didn't have to. "Doesn't mean his father did anything wrong."

"For sure, he didn't," said Fred. "Now he's a prisoner with hundreds of men. Most of them Ukrainian, too. They sleep in bunkhouses and have to work hard clearing land 'cause the government wants to test farm crops. He said it's awful thick with mosquitoes."

"That's terrible," said Peter. "I hope he can come home soon."

"Me, too," I said.

Fred's eyes was turning a bit red and shiny around the edges. He kept staring past Peter's house to Banning Street. Then he took off in that direction, saying, "Come on, let's go up the hill. Maybe we'll think of something to do on the way."

My guess was he didn't want to talk about his father anymore. Me and Peter followed him behind the houses. We tromped along a well-worn trail.

"I heard a good one the other day, Fred," I said. "Why did the suspenders get sent to jail?"

He didn't answer.

"Why?" asked Peter.

"For holding up a pair of trousers!"

Peter groaned, but Fred said nothing. He kept trudging up the path between the bushes.

Oh, that was stupid, telling a joke about jail. Quick, think of something else. I pushed a branch out of my way, then held on to it. "Hey, Peter," I said, looking back, "think fast!" I faked releasing the branch that was aimed at Peter's chest.

He flinched and jumped aside. "Hey, you brat!" said Peter, laughing. He leaped forward and tackled me to the ground in fun. We tussled and rolled, getting twigs stuck in our hair.

Fred pounced on us. He was laughing out loud, too. We wrestled until we was out of breath. Then we brushed ourselves off and carried on up the hill to a clearing.

When we reached a spot with lots of pebbles, Fred stopped. "See that big tree over there, off by itself?"

"Yeah," said me and Peter together.

"I bet I can hit it with a stone from here."

"Let's have a contest," I said. "Five stones each."

We took turns. Fred and Peter tied at four and I got only three hits.

"Okay," said Fred, "let's make it harder. We have to throw with our left hand."

Fred must've practised, 'cause he got four. Me and Peter only hit the tree twice.

We came up with more challenging shots: sitting down, then with our eyes closed, and then facing backwards. None of us hit the target that time. But we sure belly-laughed.

Fred's stomach made the loudest, growliest rumble I'd ever heard.

Me and Peter snickered.

"What?" said Fred. "There was nothing to put on my bread this morning."

"I guess your mother forgot to go shopping," said Peter.

"No, she ..." started Fred, but then his voice sounded hoarse and he turned away. "She didn't forget."

"Must be lunchtime," I said. "We best be getting home."

"Now city council's talking sense," said Papa. He was reading the newspaper and eating lunch. "They want more enemy aliens interned. With them gone, that means more jobs for the rest of us." He slurped his coffee.

"How many more do they have room for?" I asked. "Fred told me there's hundreds at Kapuskasing already."

Saara was squishing eggs into raw ground beef. She said, "What about all the immigrants like you who don't mean Canada any harm? Why should they be interned just because they were born in a certain country?"

"I meant dangerous enemy aliens," said Papa, "not regular people."

"Spies are good at pretending they're regular people," I said, jumping in before Saara could talk. "Who knows when a man might turn on Canada? I'm not talking about Fred's father, or Peter's, neither. Look down there." I pointed to the bottom of the page in Papa's hands. "It says Britain's asking the U.S. to stop German sabotagers' plots inside its borders. There've been plots to blow up ships. There've even been strikes started in plants that make war supplies for the Allies so our soldiers don't get what they need to fight. And enemy aliens already dynamited that uniform plant in south Ontario."

106

"I agree those plots need to be stopped," said Papa. "Interning suspicious enemy aliens will help do that, and putting pay packets in the hands of honest Port Arthur men is important, too." He folded the newspaper and shoved it into the woodbox.

Clunk. The letter carrier closed the lid of our mailbox. I knew Saara was waiting for mail, so I leaped out of my chair to beat her there.

"Saa-raaa," I chirped, waving an envelope in her face. "You have a letter from Mikko-o."

If she hadn't been in the middle of shaping meatballs, I'm sure she would have grabbed it from me right away. I still had a minute while she washed and dried her hands. So I held the envelope up to the light and read, "... when I get to Port Arthur on Friday, will you come with me to—"

Whoosh. She snatched her letter out of my grasp.

"—to buy an engagement ring?" I continued, faking a swoon. Papa's eyebrows shot toward the ceiling.

Saara looked mad. "It does *not* say that. You made that up. Besides, Mikko is *not* my beau—he's just a friend. He probably wants me to go with him to see that Canadian horse, Canuck, at the Northern Livery."

"So, what *does* it say, then?"

But she refused to open Mikko's letter in front of us. Instead, she shoved it in her dress pocket. Sure as snow on my birthday, I could tell she was dying to read it. Saara rushed through forming the rest of the meatballs. She quickly browned them in the frying pan.

"Come on, Saara," I teased, "don't you want to know what he wrote? Huh?"

That earned me a dark glare before she smothered the meatballs with creamy gravy and slid them in the oven. She tidied the kitchen, then raced upstairs to her bedroom. I ran after her, but she closed the door in my face.

CHAPTER 17 | Saara

"Folks who have saved up for rainy days must be pretty near broke by this time."—The Note Book, *Port Arthur Daily News*, 1915

From my dresser, I picked up Canuck—the pocket-sized Canadian horse Mikko had carved for me—and sat on my bed. If only I could be back at the North Branch farm spending time with my friends, away from my brother. Not that I wanted Aunt Marja to be sick again with tuberculosis. But I was fed up with John's taunting and mean tricks. I had to find a way to spend less time with him.

Reaching into my dress pocket, I pulled out Mikko's letter to finally read his message. My guess was wrong, too. Mikko was inviting me to meet his sister, Aleksandra, who worked as a domestic in a mansion on Court Street. He wrote, "Aleksandra she need a friend." But what sixteen-year-old young woman would want to be friends with a thirteen-year-old girl? Still, I would do this as a favour to him.

Mikko refused to take the easy way and write in Finnish. "I see you Friday, 23 July. In after noon. I am missing you." My insides fluttered. I would see him one week from today. His letter continued, "How I learn English now you are not here, Miss Mäki?" The fluttering inside me ceased. He was missing his English teacher, not his friend.

"Saara," called Mama from down the hall. "Before you take the clothes off the line and peel potatoes, I need you to deliver this suit."

Frowning, I tucked Mikko's letter in my top dresser drawer and returned Canuck to his place of honour. I'd forgotten about the clothesline. There went my plan to read my new library book. Was I never going to get a rest this summer? Before leaving Uncle's farm I'd planned to do nothing for an entire week after getting home. No chance of even a whole day!

After I ran the errand for Mama, I grabbed a laundry basket and stepped out the back door. I began reeling in the clothesline. After unpinning a pair of trousers, a dress, and two shirts, I stopped.

"That's odd," I said aloud. I'd come to a gap where something should have been pinned. I remembered making certain to hang the items almost touching so I could fit all of the wash on the line. One piece of clothing must have fallen or blown off. As I removed the rest of the clothes, I puzzled out what was missing: it was Mama's green dress.

I walked across the scrubby grass. Two clothespins lay on the ground. I picked them up, then circled the backyard. Perhaps the dress was caught in a shrub or on a tree branch.

"OW!" I yelped as I felt a sharp pain. I'd twisted my left ankle. There was a freshly dug hole in the grass and I'd tripped in it. "Who made that stupid hole?" I shouted, wincing with every other step as I hobbled back into the house. "It must have been my stupid brother!"

"Mama!" I shouted, hopping through the kitchen and falling onto a chair.

"What's wrong?" called Mama as she rushed downstairs.

"My ankle. It's sprained." As she chipped bits of ice off the block in the icebox and wrapped them in a tea towel, I explained what had happened.

"What a shame you were hurt," she said, gently placing the ice compress on my ankle. "And that my dress is gone. I haven't got time to sew another one for myself right now."

John picked that moment to enter the kitchen.

"Look what you did, pest!" I pointed at my foot.

"Saara, stop," said Mama. "I will handle this."

"What's going on?" asked John, looking bewildered.

"Are you responsible for the hole in the backyard?" asked Mama.

"You mean the one close to Fred's backyard?"

"Yes," I hissed.

"Me and Fred and Peter got bored digging a trench like the soldiers, so we decided to dig a tunnel instead, from here all the way to Peter's place, but we've got a long way to go—"

"It *is* his fault, Mama!" I said. "He probably took your dress, too, and hid it for a prank."

John screwed up his face. "I never touched nobody's dress!"

"That's *enough*, you two," said Mama. "Jussi, go fill in that hole right now and bring in the laundry. There will be no more digging except in Mrs. Entwhistle's garden. When you're done, I have some cleaning jobs for you to do."

Even though my ankle didn't feel any better, I was smiling.

The following Friday I was waiting at home for Mikko. My nerves were like a ball of wool after Sipu had batted it around. I hadn't seen Mikko in a month. He'd never been to my house. Thank goodness he'd met my family when they came to the farm or I'd have been doubly nervous.

About an hour after lunch, Mikko knocked on the door. "Hello, Saara."

As soon as he smiled, my nervousness vanished. "You found us."

"It is good Arvo drew map. This street is hiding."

"It *is* confusing. It's more a side lane than a street. Come in. Would you like some buttermilk?"

"Thank you, no. Father has only few more errands. We need see Aleksandra now."

Click. John jumped out from behind the shrub by the door, camera in hand. "What? Ain't you gonna kiss her and ask her to marry you?"

I was certain my entire face was redder than Joulupukki's fur-trimmed suit at Christmas.

Then John's right hand dove into his knickers pocket

and came out clenched. "Congratulations!" he hollered and showered us with wedding rice.

I gasped, then angrily exclaimed, "John!"

He whooped with glee.

Mikko shook rice out of his hair. "Your brother is full of surprise," he said. Then, to my relief, he laughed.

John took off. I called after him, "You'd better gather up the rice, or Mama will use the switch on your legs for wasting food." To Mikko I said, "Let's go."

When we passed Mr. Campbell working on his "farm," he glanced up. I waved and said hello. He quickly bent his head without returning my greeting. Perhaps he didn't recognize me walking with a boy.

I spoke in Finnish so Mikko could talk more freely. I explained what had happened with school and getting all of my assignments done in time. "But then my dumb brother hid my scribbler in the woodbox hoping it would get burnt to a crisp," I grumbled. "By the time I found it, I only just caught the principal before he left town. Now I'm praying he'll be pleased with my work."

"I'll pray for that, too."

"Thank you." He was the kindest boy I knew. After recounting all the other nasty pranks John had pulled on me, I said, "Did you treat Aleksandra like that when you were younger?"

"I never hurt her on purpose, but I did tease her horribly."

"Why'd you do it?"

"It was fun to see her reaction," he said with a chuckle. "She always got so mad at me."

113

"Did she ever get you back? I'm looking for ideas."

"She had her ways. I'm sure you'll think of something."

"I just don't understand John. Why the endless pranks? He must find them funny, but I sure don't."

"It could be he wishes he had a brother, so he treats you like one."

"Hmm … maybe." *But even though I've always longed for a sister, I wouldn't dream of treating John like a girl.* I wasn't sure Mikko understood how upset I was with John—perhaps it was better to change the subject.

Sweet-smelling cardamom wafted down the block from Kivelä Bakery and made my mouth water for *pulla.* We dodged shoppers laden with sacks of bread and groceries.

"Have you seen my aunt and uncle lately?" I said. "How is Sanni?"

"A few days ago I stopped by to borrow a tool. You should have seen Marja searching for Sanni. Her hair was a mess and skirts were flying." At this Mikko mussed his hair and switched to a high voice. "'Help, Sanni ran away!' Arvo and I took off to opposite ends of the farm-yard, him to check the barn, and me the garden. I found her happily raiding the strawberry patch."

I could picture her little cheeks covered in berry juice. "That was my biggest fear, that she'd get away from me and fall into the well or something else terrible."

"I remember the harness you made for her. It worked fine until she learned to undo buckles." That led to further reminiscing about my time at the farm.

We had about a block farther to walk. I should have

worn a hat—the sun beat down on us in earnest. "What did you name your colt?" I asked.

"An English name so he'll sell more easily: Blaze." Like Current River in spring, Mikko poured out his latest plans for raising Canadian horses. It took no time at all to reach the mansion where Aleksandra worked.

Mikko led me past the wide veranda and around the immense brick house to the back door—the servants' entrance. He knocked loudly.

A pretty young woman in uniform opened the door, calling over her shoulder, "I be right back. Five minutes."

"Aleksandra, this is Saara," said Mikko.

His sister abandoned English in favour of Finnish. "So this is your special friend. It's lovely to meet you finally," she said, offering her hand to shake.

I shook it firmly, as Papa had taught me. "Hello, Aleksandra. Mikko told me you have to work a lot, but would you like to go roller skating with me on your next day off?"

"That sounds exhausting. I only have every second Wednesday afternoon free and then all I want to do is rest my feet and drink coffee."

"We could see a moving picture show at one of the theatres," I offered. Being under fifteen, I couldn't legally go to picture shows unaccompanied, but with someone older I could get in.

Aleksandra smiled. "Yes, that would suit me. Can you meet me here at noon in two Wednesdays?"

"Sure."

"Aleksandra!" shouted a harsh voice through the open window. "The meat needs turning."

Seeing Mikko frown, Aleksandra reassured him, "Cook barks, but she treats me well. I have to go. I'll see you in two weeks, Saara. Goodbye." Aleksandra hurried back into the kitchen.

Mikko and I returned to the front of the mansion. "Here comes my father," he said. A horse-drawn wagon was rolling toward us. "He said he'd meet me here." The wagon was not slowing down to stop. Mikko turned to me and said, "Thank you for inviting Aleksandra out. She works too much and never mentions doing anything with a friend."

"I'll make sure to pick an exciting show."

"I'd like to see one sometime. But these trips into town are always too rushed."

"Hello, Saara, and goodbye," called Mikko's father. "We have to get back to the farm."

"See you next time, I hope," called Mikko in English, as he ran and leaped aboard the moving wagon.

As I waved, my arm knocked some rice out of my braid. That John!

CHAPTER 18 | John

"An elephant can smell a man at a distance of
1,000 yards, says an exchange. The elephant,
however, is fortunate in that it doesn't have to ride
between these two cities on a trolley car."—The Note
Book, *Port Arthur Daily News*, 1915

My ambush with rice turned out so swell, I was still
chuckling an hour later. The look on Saara's and Mikko's
faces was worth Mama getting upset at me. Now I was
lugging books home from the library.

With a block to go, Saara caught up to me.

"What's gotten into you?" she asked, pointing to my
stack of books. "Since when did you start reading apart
from homework?"

"Don't I read the newspaper through every day?" I
replied. That made her cheeks turn pink. "Shows how well
you know me, don't it?" I grunted, shifting my load. "Been
reading new books every week for months now."

That got her curious. She started listing off the titles
of my books. "*Chemistry and Chemical Magic*, boring.
Harper's Electricity for Boys, boring. *The War, 1914, for Boys
and Girls*, extremely boring." She scrunched her face as

she inspected the rest of the books in my pile. "Where are the exciting adventure stories? Or mystery books? Or even spy tales?"

"I don't want made-up stories," I said. "I want the facts and I want to write the facts."

"No, I don't know you well," she said, walking on. "I doubt I'll ever understand you."

We turned into our back lane.

"Hello, Mr. Campbell," called Saara as he looked up from watering his neat rows of vegetables.

The way he acted like we wasn't even there made my stomach do flips.

Once we was out of earshot, Saara said, "Mr. Campbell always used to talk to me."

"Yup, to me too, but not no more. I never did mischief, in case you're wondering."

Inside our house, I dumped the library books on the kitchen table with a crash.

"Quiet—Mama's trying to work," said my sister.

"Well, you could've helped me carry them."

"You never asked me to."

Before I could think of a smart comeback, Mama appeared from upstairs. "Good, you both made it here in time."

"What chore needs doing now?" Saara sighed.

Mama dug money out of the coffee-tin bank and handed it to her. "There's a sale at Chapples that cannot be missed. Take Jussi and buy him the solid leather boots—they're only a dollar ninety-five. Make sure there's plenty of growing room."

Ugh. There ain't nothing worse than shopping—'cept shopping with my sister. "My boots are just fine, Mama," I said.

As I held up my right foot, Saara stared at the crack in the sole and the split seam. She muttered under her breath, "Drat—you truly do need new boots."

Mama paid no attention to me, just kept giving orders to Saara. "Cotton crepe is only 10 cents a yard so get five yards, striped or gingham."

"Can't you take him on Saturday, Mama? You know better what fabric you need—"

"No, you must take him now—the sale is today only."

Saara groaned, so I groaned louder. We grabbed a drink of water, then retraced our steps downhill.

"You are the Biggest Pest in the World," grumbled Saara, "but at least I get a change in scenery and no back-breaking weeding or lifting or scrubbing."

Once we was on Bay Street, we saw a streetcar turn at Cumberland, coming our way. We reached the stop and the streetcar slowed.

Clang! Clang! The fire engine's bell rang out down the road.

"They're heading toward one of the grain elevators!" I yelled. "Let's follow them!"

"No, John," said Saara, but I took off anyhow. I knew she couldn't very well buy boots for me on her own, so she'd have to wait.

"Arrrg! You are a giant nuisance!" she called, running after me.

The nearest grain elevator stood solid like a castle by the water. We had nineteen of these tall storehouses in the Twin Cities. But this one had smoke rising from the base. A crowd was gathering on this side of the railway tracks. I wormed my way to the front.

"Stay back!" commanded police officers. "It could explode!"

I tapped the arm of the scrawny man next to me. "Who spotted the fire?"

"The soldier on guard patrol," he said. "Could've been started by a faulty machine inside—"

"No, it was sabotage by an enemy alien," stated the fellow beside him.

Sabotage right here? So close to our home? Bully! But I had to ask, "How do you know—?"

"Lock up all the enemy aliens!" shouted a man behind us, drowning out my question.

"Intern every last one of 'em!" said a woman's voice.

"'Tis the only way to stop the sabotage!" called someone else in the crowd.

"Clear off the road, lad," ordered one officer, directing me out of the way.

I spotted Saara on the side of the road and ran to join her.

"Lots of folks are saying a sabotager set the fire," I said.

She looked horrified.

Firemen scurried to douse the flames at the elevator.

Saara whispered, "Did you ever find out who set the fire at the *Daily News*?"

"Yup—it was a worker and they fired him. It was his cigarette butt that started the blaze. Too bad." I gave a big sigh. "It weren't sabotage, after all."

"I can't believe you're disappointed. What's wrong with you?"

The well-dressed gentleman beside me leaned toward us, saying, "This fire could destroy the whole elevator and whatever grain's in there."

"Like that elevator in Saskatchewan a few months back," piped up another man. "It burned to the ground."

"Was that from a sabotager?" I asked.

"No, lightning."

"I bet *this* is a sabotager's doing," I said.

"If it's levelled," added the gentleman, "they won't have time to rebuild for the big loads of grain coming next month."

"I don't think we need to worry about that," said Saara, pointing at the elevator.

The smoke had thinned. One fireman manned the hose while the rest stood around the engine.

"Everything's under control," shouted a policeman. "Nothing more to see."

"Let's get going, John," said my sister.

"Okay," I said with a shrug. "This ain't very exciting anymore." But I couldn't wait to get home and pull out my scribbler and pencil to get the facts down while they was fresh in my noggin. My headline would be *"FIRE, YET ELEVATOR SPARED! SABOTAGE?"* I figured raising the question was okay. But I wouldn't umbrellish the facts like Cam did to make it sound worse than it really was.

On board the streetcar, we found the last two seats together. Saara weaselled around me and took the window seat. More passengers got on. As we rolled away, I felt a big healthy belch working its way up from my gut. So I opened my mouth wide to let it rip. My sister tapped my arm and shook her head.

Then I passed gas. It was noisy, too. *Ah.*

Saara turned beet red. "John, even the conductor can hear you." She stood and scanned the jam-packed street-car. "Drat. I can't sit away from you. There's no seat free."

Oh, this was fun—she was trapped. "Saara, what's smarter than a talking monkey?" I said, snickering.

She stared out the window, refusing to answer.

"A spelling bee! How can the farmer keep his rooster from crowing in the morning?"

Saara ignored my question. But that didn't stop me.

"By having him for dinner tonight!" With each punch-line, I spoke louder and Saara's neck grew redder.

"No one else is laughing at your lame jokes," hissed Saara. "If this were a classroom and I was the teacher, you'd be staying late for a detention and writing lines."

"But this ain't a classroom." I chuckled, remembering another joke. "Here's a good one. Why should you never tell secrets in the garden? 'Cause corn has ears, potatoes got eyes, and beanstalk!"

When we changed to the Fort William streetcar, Saara tried to slip away from me by sitting next to someone else. But I grabbed the seat across the aisle from her.

"Saara," I said, tugging her sleeve, "what's white when it's dirty and black when it's clean?"

She refused to look at me.

"A blackboard!" I kept on telling my rip-roaring jokes. All too soon we reached our stop in Fort William. Saara pressed me forward as quickly as the crowd let her.

Of course, I had to try on *three* pairs of boots before Saara was satisfied. I was happy with the first ones. The checkered fabric was sold out. She picked what she called the "least ugly" striped cloth.

Finally we could leave Chapples (she made me carry the packages) and ride the streetcar back to Port Arthur. There wasn't two seats together or near each other on either part of the route, so we had to sit apart. Saara didn't seem to mind. Shucks—I couldn't tell her more jokes.

"Notwithstanding the war news, some of the old standbys are reappearing. Another sure cure for tuberculosis has been announced."—The Note Book, *Port Arthur Daily News*, 1915

John was conveniently running late selling newspapers and there I was, slaving alone in the humid garden. It wasn't that I missed him, but he was supposed to be helping. I wiped my dripping forehead and studied the weedless rows. Carrot, beet, and onion tops reached for the sun. The green peas were close to picking.

As I gathered the garden tools, John finally showed up. "You're just in time to put these away," I snarled, dumping the tools at his feet. "And I won't be helping you do the weeding next time," I added and stomped toward home.

I rounded the corner of our house to a most welcome sight: Uncle Arvo atop his wagon.

"Hello, Uncle! Are you staying or leaving?"

"Morning, Saara. I'm off to pick up supplies while you ladies visit."

I gave his workhorses, Ace and Copper, each a quick pat before dashing inside.

"Sanni bunny, where are you?" I called. The answering squeal made my heart sing.

"Awa! Awa!" yelled Sanni as she lunged for my hug. My hands were grimy, so I took care not to touch her white dress. She raised her arms, begging to be lifted up.

"Yes, Sanni, as soon as I wash off this dirt." I showed her my hands. She dragged me by the skirt to the kitchen sink. While I scrubbed, I noticed one of Auntie's small woven baskets by my elbow. It was half full with sprouting potatoes and a somewhat wizened turnip—the dregs of last summer's harvest. Still, they were welcome to stretch our food money.

Mama bustled about, preparing coffee and setting out *pulla* and cookies. I barely kept myself from grabbing a slice of the cardamom-scented bread. Clean again, I picked up Sanni and joined Aunt Marja in the parlour. When we sat on the end of the sofa closest to Auntie's chair, Sanni chortled and hugged my neck.

"I see my girl hasn't forgotten you, Saara," said Auntie. Not long ago, those words would have come out drenched in bitterness. That was when Auntie had been too sick with tuberculosis to take care of Sanni, too sick to even touch her. It had pained her deeply to see me mothering her baby.

A surprise visit could mean that my aunt was not well again. "How are you feeling? You're not here to see the doctor, are you?"

"Well, yes, I do want to see him. There's no cough or fever, just more tiredness." She leaned her head against the chair back. "Perhaps it's only from chasing Sanni, but I must know if the tuberculosis has come back. You remember my friend Josephine from the Toronto sanatorium, don't you?"

"Oh, yes. Doesn't she call her little Timmy a tornado?" I asked.

"She does. Well, on Friday I received a letter from her. Poor Josephine. She has relapsed and returned to the sanatorium." Auntie pulled her handkerchief out and dabbed her eyes. "Josephine in Toronto, and her wee Timmy off in the Preventorium in Hamilton. Now he has tuberculosis, too. The doctors want to treat him early to prevent him suffering for a long time. No, I cannot be too careful. I couldn't bear to leave my family again, or have any of you get sick."

"I don't want that either." Lowering my voice, I continued, "I want to be back at the farm with you. John is so immature. He keeps pulling hurtful pranks on me. And he always talks about how to help the war effort and imagines German spies around every corner. I miss you."

"I miss you, too," said Auntie. "Boys long for adventure, and to them, war is exactly that. Besides, don't forget how ill he's been over the years with pneumonia and such—I know how useless one feels lying in bed week after week. He wants to do all he can to help Canada win the war, I'm sure."

I hadn't thought of John's weak lungs making him want to be useful even more. I pictured his scribbler with his practice article about everyone helping the war effort. *Everyone.* Yes, growing our own food was a help. But what more could *I* do? I couldn't stop the saboteurs, but I *could* volunteer at the Red Cross room.

Mama beckoned from the kitchen doorway. "Coffee time," she said and took over the conversation.

When John brought out his camera and took two pictures of Sanni, I smiled. "That's a good idea. Thank you, John." I played with my cousin until Uncle showed up to take her and Auntie to see the doctor.

When they returned later, Aunt Marja's face glowed. "I'm fine—*perfectly* fine. Sanni's going to have a brother or sister."

"Hurrah!" I shouted. Another future pupil for North Branch. *If only I could be the North Branch teacher ... if only I could be a teacher.*

From Saturday's newspaper, I learned that the Red Cross room would be open on Monday afternoon for volunteers to prepare dressings, bandages, and hospital garments to be shipped to Toronto the following day. "Workers are always welcome," the notice said. Good—it didn't sound like they needed knitters that day. All of my attempts at knitting were pathetic.

Come Monday, I washed the laundry at high speed so that after lunch I was free to volunteer. I entered the Red Cross room and came face to face with two girls close to my age. "Name?" asked the one with raven hair.

"Saara Mäki."

She started writing my name in her book. The blonde girl snatched the pencil out of her hand, saying, "Wait a minute, Elizabeth. She doesn't have a patriotic button."

Elizabeth looked puzzled. "She doesn't need a button to volunteer, Margaret."

"Oh, yes, *she* does." Margaret's eyes blazed at me from below her yellowish bangs.

I looked at the girl again, surprised at the anger in her voice. She was missing her bright skirt, beads, and head scarf, but I recognized her now. She was one of the gypsy girls from the Red Cross garden party.

"*Germans* aren't welcome." Margaret spewed her barbed words, then sneered.

"For your information, I'm a Canadian," I said, standing tall, "and besides, according to the Red Cross notice, *everyone* is welcome."

"It does say that, Margaret," said Elizabeth.

"I guess she can stay," huffed Margaret, "this time."

Elizabeth smiled at me, saying, "The convenor will find a spot at a table for you." She pointed to the lady standing near the four Singer sewing machines. Lowering her voice, she added, "Don't mind Margaret—come back anytime."

"Oh, hello, miss," said the convenor. "I have one vacancy at a sewing machine. Are you able to sew?"

I shook my head. Mama's sewing machine and I did not get along. "I'm handy with a pair of scissors."

"Wonderful. Over here we are preparing antiseptic dressings from hospital gauze," she said, walking toward a large table in the corner.

Once I was seated, the lady on my right gave me instructions. During the next two hours we made dozens of dressings of all sizes and rolled a whole bolt of cotton into bandages. Being productive like this felt soothing. These pieces of fabric could make all the difference in keeping wounded soldiers alive.

Food prices were rising, and so was the tension in our household. When Mama served only rice pudding for supper once a week instead of meat and potatoes, I knew she was getting worried about money. Due to Papa's attempts to organize a union, his boss cut his hours. And Mama had fewer sewing jobs. Wartime caused people to hang on to their money and make do. Or stop hiring foreigners, like Mrs. Brooks had done, at her husband's insistence.

Mama had a bit of time now to cook. I still had to help with preparing meals, plus wash dishes, clean, do the gardening, and run errands with John. When we worked together, he drove me crazy with his silliness and loafing; when he wasn't around, I resented all the free time he had to do whatever he wished.

After breakfast on Tuesday, Mama said, "Saara, the kitchen floor needs scrubbing," and then she settled into her sewing upstairs. Down on my hands and knees, I pushed and pulled the soapy floor rag from one end of the room to the other. By the time I finished, my back was aching, so I stretched out on the sofa to rest.

John slammed the door on his way in. Before I could warn him away from the wet floor, he slipped and banged his knee against the wood stove. He cussed with a word I'd never heard come out of him. Seeing me in the doorway, he said, "How come you didn't warn me it was slippery?"

"How come you didn't check first? Look at the muddy tracks you made. Now I have to redo the floor." I kept my voice low so Mama wouldn't hear. "No, I have a better idea. You can wash the floor this time."

If John had walked a block in a blizzard, his face wouldn't have been brighter red. "I wish you was back at the farm and out of my hair! I liked it better when you wasn't around."

"I wish I didn't have to spend *any* time with you. Who says I like being around someone who whines and tries to get out of chores?"

"Stop treating me like a baby!" he shouted.

I heard Mama walking toward the top of the stairs. In a loud whisper, I told John, "There you go, interrupting Mama's work *again*."

He made a face.

Mama called down to us, "What's going on?"

"We're just talking," I answered.

"Keep the noise down or go outside," Mama said, returning to her sewing machine.

John growled, "I'm not a little kid anymore—I'm earning money for the family and you ain't."

"When I start working as a teacher, I'll give some of my wages to the family."

"I feel sorry for any kids who get *you* for a teacher. Miss Pritchard is *nice* compared to you."

That stung worse than iodine in an open cut. Students at our school dreaded getting assigned to Miss Pritchard's classroom. Hearing Papa come into the house didn't stop me from spewing, "I hope you get Miss Pritchard in September and she's in a bad mood all year!"

John grabbed a piece of kindling and hurled it straight at my legs, nicking my shin. I screamed. A spot of blood appeared.

"Stop your fighting!" commanded Papa.

"We ain't fighting," said John.

Papa picked up the kindling. "Don't tell me throwing this and hurting your sister isn't fighting," he said, his voice stern. "Jussi, go to your room and stay there for the rest of the day. Saara, leave your brother alone."

Obeying my father would not be a problem.

CHAPTER 20 | John

"While it is wrong to hate our enemies, most of us put strict limits on our enthusiasm for the Germans."—The Note Book, *Port Arthur Daily News*, 1915

Good thing Papa only said I had to stay in my room until the end of yesterday. 'Cause I had an important job to do this morning. Peter wanted to be a newsboy, too, so I was gonna teach him.

I stepped outside and bumped right into early-bird Fred. "Before you get Peter," he said, "I ... uh ... I need to know something."

"Sure. What?"

"Is there enough work for all of us? What if I can't sell my usual number of papers? I ... uh ... really need the money, Johnny."

"Didn't you notice? Those two brothers with the suspenders that started last week never came back after Sunday."

"Oh, yeah? I guess there's room for one more." He sounded relieved. "Let's get him."

I tapped on the front door at Peter's house. After a minute, he showed up, yawning.

Giving him a friendly punch in the arm, I said, "You'll get used to getting up so early."

We beat the other fellows to the *Daily News* building, got our papers, and me and Peter set up at my corner. After stacking the papers at our feet, I snatched the top one and unfolded it to see the whole front page.

"First off," I said, "you've got to read enough to know what's big news today. That's how you work out your pitch."

"Pitch? What is that?" asked Peter, looking confused.

"What you're going to holler to get people to buy the paper. Let's see, today's top headline is *WAR HAS BECOME A CONTEST OF ENDURANCE*. That ain't going to sell many papers."

"What are we going to do?"

"We have to dig deeper and find something more interesting to get people's attention." I scanned the front page.

A tiny notice caught my eye. It read, "Friday's elevator fire was caused by a spark from a machine igniting the grain dust." So it wasn't sabotage, after all. I kept searching for a better headline.

"Peter, here's one: *FRENCH WIN ANOTHER BIG SUCCESS!* And here's another: *MORE CENSORSHIP FOR NEWSPAPERS*." I read further. "And what's inside that bit about censorship is interesting. Newspapers gave away military secrets. They shouldn't have printed this, but they did, so we can use it: *WAVE PAINTED ON BRITISH BATTLESHIP MEANT TO DECEIVE GERMANS*. Those two together will sell papers, you'll see."

I refolded the paper, grabbed one more, and shoved it into Peter's hands. "Hold it up like this." I showed him how, then bellowed the censorship and painted wave pitch to the folks approaching us, followed by, "Read all about it!"

Both men bought a copy.

"Okay, Peter. Your turn."

"*MORE CENSORSHIP! WAVE ON BATTLESHIP MEANT TO DECEIVE GERMANS!*" he said at normal volume.

"Be sure you say *WAVE PAINTED*, okay? And louder this time. You have to make those people coming toward us stop talking and look at you."

He raised his voice and got their attention, but he faded out on the last word. It was okay, though, 'cause they'd already decided to buy.

"Rats," he said. "Both of my pockets have holes. Can you hold these for me?" He gave me the coins. With the next person, he had trouble shouting the last word again. That man didn't want a newspaper.

Peter hung his head. "I can't do this, John."

"It's okay. He walks by every day and never buys a paper from me."

"No, it's saying the *Germans* part. I don't want Germany to win the war—I wish there wasn't a war at all—but it's hard for me to shout about them losing."

"Yeah, that's tough. But if you're going to do this—"

"You have to pitch the news," finished a familiar voice. I looked up. It was Ricky, one of the older newsboys. He'd already sold out of his papers. "Why's it hard for you when they're losing?" He nosed in close to Peter. "You ain't a Hun, are you?"

"Yes, I-I-I am," said Peter, so quietly I hardly heard him.

"We'll see what the boss at the *Daily News* has to say about that."

"Ricky, leave him be," I said. "He's rooting for us in the war."

"From what I heard, I'm not so sure about that," said Ricky, marching away.

"Don't worry about him, Peter," I said, trying to sound confident. "He won't do anything."

By the time we got to the last of our papers, Peter was hooting and hollering like the best of the newsboys.

CHAPTER 21 | Saara

"Another thing that contradicts the hard times
stories is the number of ads for servant girls."
—The Note Book, *Port Arthur Daily News*, 1915

After John got home from delivering papers, Mama sent
us to the Co-Op with a long list. I managed to get all the
shopping done without saying one word to him.

As soon as the handcart was loaded, my wood-
throwing brother said, "Botheration—I forgot to give
something to Peter. It's important. You can manage the
cart, right?"

Rude John didn't wait for my answer but ran off, leaving me to haul the groceries home on my own. Something important. Ha! I didn't believe him for a second.
He just wanted to get out of this chore. At least the cart
wasn't nearly as heavy as the time it tipped.

As I dragged the cart from Secord Street into our
back lane, I thought of a brilliant plan. If I found a job,
I could bring in money for my family, too. And it would
give me hours and hours a week away from the Pest.

At home, I fished today's newspaper out of the woodbox and turned to the Help Wanted column.

Wanted—Young girl to assist with housework. Apply Mrs. Prescott, 70 S. Cumberland Street. Too far from home.

Wanted—General Servant, 24 College Street. Apply evenings. To work for people on College Street I was sure I'd have to wear a prissy uniform. No, thank you.

Wanted—Two teachers for Schools No. 1 and No. 2. Someday that would be the job for me. Maybe. My pulse quickened. What had Mr. Graham thought of my work? Surely he approved and would promote me to Senior Fourth. It was almost August—I should hear from him soon.

Wanted—Young girl to care for baby a few hours each day. Phone 2032 North. No address. How could I phone without a telephone? I didn't even know anyone with a telephone.

WANTED AT ONCE—Girl for light housework … That sounded good. *… one who can milk.* Yes, that was me! *No washing.* I liked that. *Mrs. Richmond, 337 Van Norman Street.* It was perfect.

After eating lunch and cleaning up the kitchen, I washed my face and changed into a fresh dress. Then I re-braided my hair. Without breathing a word to Mama, I headed out to apply.

My fresh dress was limp by the time I knocked on the door, despite the cooler weather. Thank goodness it hadn't started to rain yet.

A tall woman opened the door, saying a tired hello. Judging by the bulge beneath her apron, she was expecting a baby.

"Are you Mrs. Richmond?" She nodded. "I've come

to answer your ad." Silence. I continued, "To do light housework?"

She picked up one of my braids and inspected my homemade dress. Her gaze lingered on my shoes. *Drat.* I'd forgotten to polish them. Finally she spoke. "Your age?"

"Thirteen, ma'am."

"I am looking for someone older, more responsible."

"Oh, I'm quite responsible. Looked after my aunt's baby and household while she was ill. And I can milk."

"No, thank you. Goodbye," Mrs. Richmond said and closed the door in my face.

Didn't she believe me? I should have said I was fourteen. I was certainly tall enough to fool people. From my dress pocket I pulled out the list of ads I'd clipped from the newspaper. I reconsidered the College Street job. *Apply evenings.* By the time I walked there, it would be late afternoon. That was almost evening. I spat into my handkerchief and used it to scrub the worst of the dirt from my shoes.

A light drizzle began when I was a block away. I speed-walked, not wanting to run and get out of breath. Once at the house, I climbed the steps, lifted the heavy knocker, and let it bang. There was no sound from inside. I banged the knocker twice. Now there were footsteps. The woman of the house looked a bit dishevelled, like she'd just awoken from a nap. She mumbled, "Yes?"

"Hello. I've come about the general servant job."

"My husband conducts the interviews—in the *evenings.* Are you not able to read?"

"Yes, I can read quite well. I'm sorry. I thought it would be later by the time I walked here."

"You'll have to come back after six o'clock." She yawned. "Actually, don't bother to come back. We don't hire foreigners." She slammed the door before I could tell her I was born in Canada. I crumpled my list and pitched the wad at the closed door. Stomping down the stairs and back to the street, I wondered how long it would take me to get hired. I hadn't realized it would be so difficult.

The next day's paper contained mostly the same ads, but with one addition. *Wanted—General servant for family of two.* That sounded all right. *Must speak English.* Definitely. *Must be good plain cook.* Plain cooking I could easily do. *Phone 1587 North. Mrs. Douglas McLeod, 100 Summit Avenue.* That was right up the hill. *Only competent need apply.* After all my experience at the farm, Competent was my middle name.

I remembered the College Street woman's comment: "We don't hire foreigners." Why had she thought I was a foreigner? Unlike my parents, I had no Finnish accent. I didn't think I looked any different from my friends with English parents, except for my braids. That was easily fixed. I loosened my braids and brushed my wavy hair until it shone. Deception number one. Wearing my best dress, I set off.

As I hiked up to Summit Avenue, I rehearsed my lines to persuade Mrs. McLeod to hire me. "My specialty is plain beef stew and plain homemade bread." "I've had many months' experience looking after a young child." The breeze flung long strands of my hair into my face.

Combing it back with my fingers, I missed how braids corralled my hair. "I am very competent." "I get top marks on my English compositions."

Summit Avenue was newly developed and lined with mansions. I found the address and nervously crossed the veranda to knock on the door. The lady of the house opened it immediately. Her face was as perfectly smooth as Birgitta's porcelain dolls.

"Good morning, Mrs. McLeod," I said confidently. "I am very competent and cook plainly and want to work for you." That didn't come out as rehearsed, but at least she was smiling.

"Well, the ad must have been printed today as promised. Tell me your name."

"Saara Mäki, ma'am," I said, pronouncing my first name the Canadian way (instead of *Sah-ra*) and my last name like my Senior Third teacher's name, Mr. McKee. Deception number two.

"And Sarah McKee, how old are you?"

"Fourteen, ma'am." Deception number three really made me squirm, but I wanted so badly to get this job. "I know how to care for young children."

"That is wonderful, dear, but there are no children in this house … yet. Only the two of us, Mr. McLeod and myself."

I was worried I'd embarrassed her, but she still sounded warm and friendly.

"Can you start right away?" she asked. I nodded. "I'd intended to properly interview applicants, but I'm in a pinch. I invited my cousin for tea today, completely oblivious to it being the last Thursday of the month, which means the Red Cross meeting is this afternoon. You can begin in the parlour. This way." The skirt of her dress swished around to follow her past the entrance to the cavernous parlour.

I'd done it! I was actually an official general servant now. Passing this hurdle made my guilty feelings fade. Once Mrs. McLeod saw my competent work, it wouldn't matter what or who I had pretended to be.

"Here you are, Sarah," she said, opening a hall closet neatly stocked with cleaning supplies. "After you finish dusting the parlour, run the vacuum cleaner over the floor; you'll find it in the corner there." She pointed to farther inside the closet. "I shall be upstairs in the library preparing my talk for the meeting, should you need anything."

Vacuum cleaner? I'd heard of them but had never seen one. And library? Who had a *library* in their house? I wasn't simply in another neighbourhood—a rich one, to be sure—I was on a different planet.

Mrs. McLeod's shoes tap-tap-tapped the shiny wood steps on her way up to the library. I grabbed a dusting cloth and dampened it at the kitchen sink, noting the brand new electric stove. Carefully lifting the crystal vase of cut flowers off the parlour table, I wiped its smooth square surface. The room had so much empty space it felt as if furniture was missing, yet there was twice the amount that was crammed into our parlour. I worked my way from sofa to side table to large cupboard to armchair, ending up staring out the picture window.

Against the bold blue sky, Lake Superior sparkled like a jewel. The Sleeping Giant rock formation seemed larger, more crisply outlined than ever before.

"Tsk, tsk, girl," said Mrs. McLeod. I spun to see her in the doorway, one hand on her hip, the other holding a glass of water with ice. "I am not paying you to lollygag and enjoy the view, Miss McKee. Mind your duties."

"I'm sorry, ma'am. It won't happen again." She returned upstairs while I quickly finished dusting. Back at the hall closet, I wrestled the unwieldy vacuum cleaner from its storage spot into the parlour. It stood upright with a long handle, suspended bag, and wide, low nozzle. I unwound the cord, then stood on a chair below the light fixture, hunting for its electrical outlet. I wasn't sure I could reach to attach the plug if I did find it. No. I was going to have to admit to Mrs. McLeod I needed help. I set down the cord and headed upstairs. The library was directly above the parlour. I found Mrs. McLeod primly sitting at a desk, writing rapidly.

"Pardon me, ma'am."

"What is it?"

"I'm ready to use the vacuum cleaner, but I can't locate the outlet."

"That's because I cleverly concealed it," she said with a chuckle. "Look behind the Louis the Fifteenth armchair." She returned to her writing.

I didn't know what a first Louis armchair looked like, let alone a fifteenth, and was too embarrassed to ask. There weren't that many armchairs in the parlour. Surely I could find the outlet. Beginning with the largest chair,

I found the outlet behind the third armchair. I inserted the plug and the machine roared to life, startling me. Nowhere on the base was an on-off switch. Fine, I would get busy cleaning. When I grabbed the handle, my hand brushed a knob that rotated and silenced the vacuum cleaner. Ah—what a day of discoveries. I restarted the vacuum cleaner and pushed it forward, guiding the nozzle around the legs of the furniture.

Pushing worked well on the hardwood floor but kept bunching the carpet, so I switched to pulling the machine along. With my back to the door, I concentrated on collecting every speck of dust.

Someone tapped me on the shoulder. Startled, I sidestepped. My foot caught in a fold of the rug and I dropped the handle, which bumped into the parlour table, tipping the vase and bouquet onto the floor. The roar of the vacuum cleaner hid the sound of smashing glass, but not the horror.

I turned the knob on the handle to shut off the machine.

"What a shame—that's her special one," said a man's voice.

I whipped around.

A man in a suit stood there, his bowler hat in hand. He smoothed his inky black hair, then said, "Mr. Douglas McLeod, here, and you are?"

"Sarah, sir, and I'm terribly sorry, sir." I began to scoop up the broken glass and scattered flowers.

"Douglas? Is that you, darling?" called Mrs. McLeod on her way downstairs.

"Yes—I'm only here for a minute. I forgot an important paper for work."

"Good—I'll ride with you downtown, then." Mrs. McLeod entered the parlour, spotted the glass shards, and exclaimed, "Not my precious vase!"

"Now, dear, it wasn't entirely Sarah's fault. I surprised her."

I deposited the wreckage in the kitchen garbage, then snatched a rag and started mopping the floor.

"I-I suppose it could happen to anyone," said Mrs. McLeod, "but still, the replacement cost will need to come out of her wages."

The word I muttered under my breath was not English. It was Finnish and it wasn't polite. I'd learned too many of those words from the boarders at Helena's.

"What did you say?" Mrs. McLeod's puzzled face stared at me.

I had to think quickly. "I said, 'I owe you.' I agree that I owe you for the vase."

"It is good to take responsibility. But how unfortunate. I brought that piece of crystal all the way from England."

I wanted to scream. How long would it take me to work off my debt?

"Well, do try to be more careful, won't you?" she said.

"I'll retrieve my paper and wait for you in the motorcar, dear," said her husband, waving on his way out.

"Sarah, I want to give you the instructions for preparing tea before I leave. Come to the kitchen."

I was about to tell her I knew how to brew tea, when

she thrust a newspaper clipping into my hands. "I want you to assemble this Butterfly Salad for our tea."

I stared at the recipe title in disbelief. My employer must be insane. *Butterfly* Salad? I didn't know anyone ate butterflies.

"Is something wrong, Sarah?"

"Where is the net I'll need to catch the butterflies?"

Mrs. McLeod laughed so hard she snorted. "Oh, Sarah. Your funny bone is in tip-top shape." She paused, taking in my expression. "You *can* read, can't you?"

"Yes, ma'am," I said and read aloud the name of the recipe and number of servings.

"Go on."

"Remove all skin from two …" I began, my stomach threatening to empty. My legs wanted to bolt.

"Two?"

I didn't know if I could continue, but somehow I did. "… two grapefruit and three Sunkist oranges and cut into uniform slices across the fruit, and then into halves." I skimmed to the end of the instructions and exclaimed in relief, "Oh—it's not real butterflies, only meant to *look* like butterflies."

Mrs. McLeod simply shook her head and said good-bye. I wondered if she was the type to endlessly tease people like Richard did.

After stowing the vacuum cleaner in the hall closet, I set to work skinning the grapefruit, trying to keep the segments intact. Neither Mama nor Aunt Marja would ever prepare a dish so fiddly. Besides, we never ate salad at home—always cooked vegetables. Once I finished skinning and slicing the fruit, I shredded the lettuce and made a nest on each plate. I placed two grapefruit pieces in the centre of each nest, their curved sides touching. Next came half slices of pineapple, then the orange segments. After searching the kitchen I found pimento and placed a strip as the "body" of each butterfly, with a nut meat for the head. There was still an hour before I was expected to serve tea. I decided not to pour on the dressing yet.

By the time Mrs. McLeod arrived, I had the table set for tea and the teapot warming.

"Oh, my," she gushed. "The butterflies are gorgeous, pet."

She said it without a touch of teasing, not even a wink. I breathed easier, saying, "Thank you, ma'am."

I completed the preparations for tea a few minutes before the door knocker tapped. Remembering how Mrs. Brooks's inferior domestic answered the door, I welcomed Mrs. McLeod's cousin with a flourish. Between oohs and aahs over the salad, she tittered at everything my employer said.

Mrs. McLeod kept me busy polishing silverware while they ate. Then I would have to wash their dishes and prepare supper. How different it felt getting paid to peel a potato. Well, I wasn't being paid yet. How much did a crystal vase cost?

CHAPTER 22 | John

"Spending a little less than we earn would be easy if we could get into the habit of wanting a little less than we can afford."—The Note Book, *Port Arthur Daily News,* 1915

I wished I had an Extra to sell. When I opened Mama's coffee-tin bank this morning to stash my earnings, there was less money inside than usual. What else could I do to earn some cash? Supper wouldn't be for a couple of hours, so I headed down to Bay Street.

First stop: the Coca-Cola bottling works. I found the Coca-Cola man in the rear of the building. "Hello—have you got any small jobs I can do for you today?"

"Come back when you're a couple of feet taller and have some real muscle."

At the Co-Op, the clerk said, "Did you forget something earlier?"

"No, I got everything on the shopping list." Mama had thought of a few more groceries to buy today. She'd wanted Saara to go, but my sister was nowhere to be found after breakfast. I hadn't minded running the errand. "Is the manager here?"

"He's in the back."

The manager had me sweep the storeroom and then paid me two whole cents. It was a great start. Back outside, the wind picked up and blew grit in my face. The barber shop doorway had piles of litter and dirt. That gave me an idea.

I stepped inside, where the barber was lathering a man's chin getting ready to give him a shave. "Excuse me—will you pay me a penny to sweep out front?"

"Go ahead, boy. Broom'n dustpan're over there," he said, pointing to the corner.

In no time I had his doorway swept clean and dumped the garbage and dirt in his bin in the back lane. I repeated my pitch at the drugstore, confectionaries, watchmaker, restaurants, and pool rooms but skipped the livery. When I headed home for supper, my pocket was jingling with coins. I was right proud to hear them tumble into the coffee-tin bank. I had worked up a thirst and poured myself a glass of milk.

"Saara? Is that you?" called Mama from the second floor.

"No, it's me," I replied.

"Where is that girl?" She did not sound happy as she came down the stairs. "If we're going to eat supper, I'll have to leave my sewing and get started on it now."

"Can I do something?"

Mama smiled. "Thank you, Jussi. You can scrub half a dozen potatoes."

There was only two left in the cupboard, so I fetched more from the cold cellar. I was washing spud number five when Saara walked in.

"Where have you been all day?" demanded Mama.

"At work," she said.

"Work? What work?" Mama crossed her arms. "I had to deliver garments myself, and Jussi did the shopping alone." I pretended to faint from exhaustion.

"I know we need more money," said Saara, "so I'm working for the McLeods up on Summit."

"You're not old enough to be a domestic."

"Mrs. McLeod hired me as a general servant."

I murmured in English, "Bet you lied about your age," then kept scrubbing.

"Mrs. McLeod is happy with my work," said Saara. Then she made a face at me.

"Job or no job, you still need to help around here," said Mama, handing her a knife and a turnip. Then she said in a nice way, "The money will surely help."

Saara grinned. "Did I get any mail today?"

"Oooh—like a love letter from Mikko-o?" I asked.

"No, pest. Like a letter from Mr. Graham."

Mama shook her head. "Not today."

Later, during supper, Saara said, "People up the hill have strange appetites."

Mama asked, "What do you mean?"

"Today I had to catch butterflies and make them into salad."

"Ew!" I said. "That's disgusting. Rich folk is loony. Regular meat is fine with me."

CHAPTER 23 | Saara

"'No Germans need apply' sounds to us like a safe and sane slogan for employers of labour in Canada."—The Note Book, *Port Arthur Daily News*, 1915

On my way to the McLeods' early the next morning, I crested the hill and stopped in my tracks. A young bull moose stood at the edge of Mariday Park. He was a statue, watching me with half-chewed grass hanging from his mouth. I remained still, returning the animal's stare. When he looked away, I hurried to the McLeods' home so I wouldn't be late for work.

"Good morning, ma'am," I said, then noticed Mr. McLeod and added, "Sir."

"Good morning, Miss McKee." In a stern tone he said, "Mrs. McLeod is in charge of the help, so you listen to her. There will be no sweet-talking in my direction hoping for an increase in wages." Then he smiled and added, "You're a tad too thin, but my wife tells me you worked hard." Mr. McLeod got to his feet, pecked his wife's cheek, and centred his bowler on his head. "I'm off to run my kingdom, dear."

"Ta-ra, darling," said Mrs. McLeod. After her husband closed the front door, she asked me, "Do I recall correctly that you have experience caring for babies?"

"Lots and lots, ma'am."

"Splendid. Mrs. Stafford and I wish to explore the shops unencumbered, so she will leave her wee lad here in your care. Until she arrives, you will clean up the breakfast table, then continue polishing the silverware."

"Yes, ma'am." I missed Sanni terribly, so I welcomed my morning's task. Just as I'd finished all three sizes of forks (wasn't one all you needed?), Mrs. Stafford blew in, filling the house with chatter.

"Where is the girl? Are you certain she knows proper infant care? I won't leave Calvin with just anyone."

"You're welcome to quiz her to your heart's content," said Mrs. McLeod, "as long as it doesn't take all morning."

Mrs. Stafford placed her son in my arms and proceeded to grill me on feeding, burping, wrapping, diaper changes, napping, colic, and rashes. All the while little Calvin snuggled contentedly.

Satisfied with my answers, she said, "Well, then, let's be off."

Later, once I'd warmed Calvin's bottle and fed him, he required a great deal of rocking and singing to settle. It was time for his morning nap. I retrieved his blanket from the sofa and laid him inside his carriage. I rolled the carriage to the shady side of the veranda and secured the brakes. While he slept in the fresh air, I returned to my silverware polishing.

A bell rang in the parlour, making me jump and drop

a spoon. It jangled across the floor. I retrieved the half-polished spoon and left the kitchen to investigate. The second ring helped me locate the source. It was the telephone. I only knew what one looked like; I'd never operated one. I needed to ask Mrs. McLeod how to answer a call. After it was done ringing, I completed the remaining silverware.

When it was time to prepare lunch according to Mrs. McLeod's written instructions, I checked on Calvin. He snuffled a bit but slept soundly on.

I was slicing bread when the front door flew open and I dropped the knife.

"Sarah, what were you thinking leaving the baby outside?" demanded Mrs. McLeod.

"My family always does that."

Mrs. Stafford hustled inside carrying Calvin. She was livid, her face blotchy. "Are you a barbarian? There could be wild animals about!"

My knees quivered.

"Well? Explain yourself," she demanded.

"Fresh-air naps are a Finnish custom, very healthy."

"You're a Finlander?" screamed Mrs. Stafford. Calvin howled.

"Yes," I replied in a quiet voice.

"I entrusted my child to the care of a socialist alien!" she cried.

Mrs. McLeod's eyes widened in shock. "You deceived me, Sarah McKee, or is that even your real name? You're fired. Leave at once."

"But I need to work to pay for—"

"Forget about that. Just go. Mr. McLeod and I don't ever want to see you again."

I scuttled out the door, ran over to my lookout spot, and sat on my favourite rock slab, tears flowing. What would I say to my family? No more job; no money earned at all. I dreaded Mama's shame. Papa's disapproval. John's taunting. I could not tell them. I'd have to pretend to go to work every day until I found another job.

Mama was surprised to see me home so soon, but I convinced her that Mrs. McLeod had kindly let me go early.

"And she gave me Sundays off, too," I lied. That meant a normal Sunday and I didn't need to go job hunting. Besides, there'd be no new ads because no newspaper was printed on Sunday.

I heated leftovers, set the table, and sliced rye bread. Everything was ready when Papa got home, so we started without John. I was grateful my parents had plenty to talk about between themselves.

"*ON THE LOOSE!*" hollered John, barging in and interrupting our meal. "*CARL SCHMIDT ESCAPES FROM JAIL!*" Mama gasped. John waved a copy of the Extra.

"How did he escape?" asked Papa.

"I haven't heard. No one at the *Daily News* knows yet."

"What will he try to sabotage next?" I said.

"I wonder if he'll stay in Port Arthur," said John. "Or will he try again to blow up the bridge in Nipigon?"

Mama pressed her hands together, saying, "May God help the police find him quickly."

Saturday morning's newspaper had only one new want ad. Neatly dressed, I set out to apply for the new job and for all the others in longer-running ads I hadn't yet answered. By the afternoon I'd finished my list. I tried every hotel within walking distance, too, with no success. I was worn out, still unemployed, and starving, but I couldn't return home. On Monday I'd need to sneak some bread and cheese.

Later, back at my house, I guzzled two glasses of water and chomped a thick piece of buttered rye bread.

Mama said, "Don't ruin your appetite for supper."

I almost laughed, then said, "I worked hard today."

"What did you cook this time?" asked John. "Caterpillars or worms?"

It sounded like he'd figured out I had been stringing him along. "Neither—it was frogs."

"Yum-yum. Fried or boiled?"

"Raw with lemon juice!"

"EEEEW!"

Mrs. McLeod's ad returned to the Help Wanted column on Monday. So no one else would see it, I clipped it along with all the new ads, and then I stashed the newspaper in the middle of the pile in the woodbox. I stuffed a piece of rye bread in my pocket. From the icebox I scrounged the last bit of homemade squeaky cheese.

I followed up every new ad. First I trudged up to a house near Prospect School. Then I made my way to a couple of homes in the neighbourhood near our church. It was another long day of no's.

A glint of metal in the weeds caught my eye. I stooped to get a closer look. There lay an emerald bracelet! If the gems were real, the bracelet would be worth lots of money. Had a reward been posted? The only way to know would be to check this morning's newspaper—but it was too early for me to return home.

Picking up the bracelet, I thought hard, trying to figure out where I could look at a paper. I couldn't very well knock on a stranger's door and ask to see their *Daily News*.

Then a brilliant idea came to me. I could go directly to the *Daily News* and ask. With my spirits high, I trekked to the newspaper office. At the front desk, I asked the clerk, "Were there any notices for lost jewellery today?"

"I'll check." She flipped to the classifieds. "Yes, there's a reward for a silver brooch and an emerald bracelet."

"How do I claim the one for the bracelet?" I asked, holding up the found jewellery.

"Right here," said the clerk, reaching for the bracelet. *Hurrah!*

"Where did you find it?" she asked.

"On Park, near Cumberland, lying in the weeds beside a fence."

"The owner will be overjoyed. Thank you for returning it. Here is your reward," she said, passing me a small but heavy packet.

"You're welcome and thank you." Once I left the building, I peeked inside and counted the coins. One fifty-cent piece and five dimes! With a skip in my step, I covered the route home in no time.

In the kitchen, I said, "Mama, hold out your hand." Keeping back two dimes to pay for a couple of shows, I pressed the rest of the coins into her palm. Mama's eyes widened. I said, "I got paid early."

She hugged me tightly. "I'm so proud of how hard you're working to help out our family."

Now John wasn't the only one who added to the coffee-tin bank. I almost broke down, though, and confessed. Would I ever find another job?

After supper, John followed me upstairs. "Didn't you say you're working for Mrs. McLeod on Summit?" he asked.

"Yes, she's a demanding boss."

He pulled a folded piece of newsprint from his pocket and spread it flat. "Then how come she still wants to hire a general servant?"

My jaw dropped. I had to think quickly. I couldn't let John give me away. "She ... she must have forgotten to cancel her ad. These rich people have money to throw away on things they don't need." There was a nervous edge to my laugh.

"Saara, you ain't foolin' me. I saw you by the *Daily News* building today, and you wasn't doing Mrs. McLeod's shopping."

My heart sank. "You're right. I'm not working for the McLeods anymore. But you ... you can't tell anyone ... please ..."

"I'm telling Mama. It's no fair you getting to laze around and me having to do all the work in that jungle of a garden."

"You can't tell her. You tried to ruin school for me, and now you'll ruin this."

"I did not try to ruin your school and I am so telling Mama."

"No, please don't," I pleaded. "I'm trying to find another job. I'm sure I'll get one."

John didn't respond.

I had to come up with something convincing. "Look, I'll do your share of the garden work, okay?"

"For the whole rest of the summer," he bargained.

"Uh, I guess so," I said, regretting my offer right away.

"Okay, I won't say anything," promised John.

Oh, how I loathed my brother.

Despite all my efforts to find work on Tuesday, I did not find a job. Thank goodness I could look forward to one pleasant event: going to the moving picture show with Aleksandra tomorrow. Back at home, I set to work helping Mama prepare supper.

The next morning I had no new want ads to follow up on, and I couldn't face wandering downtown pretending to look for work. Instead I hurried through the gardening, then knocked on Birgitta's door. She opened it, broom in hand.

"Saara, come in. Where have you been the past week?"

I longed to tell my friend everything but didn't want anyone else to hear. "Where's your family?"

"Mutti took Peter to get a tooth pulled, and Vati is looking for work, as usual."

"That's what I've been doing, too." I told her about my fiasco at the McLeods' and my secret hunt for a replacement job. I decided to keep my uncertainty about school to myself. If only Mr. Graham would send a letter to say all was well.

"Why not tell your parents the truth about your job? They will understand, no?"

"I don't know. I'd hate to let Mama down. She's counting on my earnings. None of the hotels will hire me. Some asked my age. I won't lie again—it's not worth it. Others demanded to know my ethnic background."

"Yes—as soon as the hiring boss hears Vati speak, SLAM goes the door. He *must* get work soon. Mr. Campbell is our new landlord and he just raised the rent. Vati thinks he is trying to get rid of us. I might have to join you looking for a job."

"Good luck," I said, trying to sound encouraging in the face of harsh reality. "Say, would you like to come with Mikko's sister and me to the Gaiety Theatre this afternoon? We're seeing *The Girl Detective*, 'full of hair-raising scenes.'" Remembering I had enough money for two tickets, I said, "And it would be my treat."

"I would like to go. But I have to mind my brother and sister."

"Little brothers—what bothers. Say, I need a place to kill a couple of hours. Do you mind if I stay here?"

"That is okay. I like having a cleaning partner," she said, handing me the broom.

I pitched in to help her clean the house. It was better than hunting for a job, and it took my mind off John and not hearing from Mr. Graham.

We chatted as we shook the mats outside. Then

Birgitta fell silent. "What is it?" I asked. "Did I do something wrong?"

"No. It is my uncle." Tears welled in her eyes. "This afternoon Mutti will visit with him one last time before he is sent to the camp at Kapuskasing tonight."

"Oh, Birgitta, I didn't know he was being interned." I hugged my friend.

"Yes, him and several other men, Germans and Ukrainians. What if they send Vati away? How will we survive? I heard Mutti say if he does not find work soon, she will need to sell her Omi's filigree necklace to pay our rent."

"They wouldn't intern your father. He's done nothing wrong." Even as I said it, I remembered what had happened to Fred's father.

"I do not think my uncle did anything wrong."

"I'm sorry—I didn't mean to say he did."

Birgitta mumbled, "I know" and pulled out her handkerchief to wipe her eyes and blow her nose. She replaced the mats while I started dusting.

When we finished her list of chores, Birgitta fetched a deck of cards and we played All-Fours until it was time for me to leave to meet Aleksandra.

"I hope you find a job tomorrow," said Birgitta.

"Me, too. But if I don't, can I come back here?"

"You do not need to ask," she said, giving me a hug. "You are always welcome here."

I felt lucky to have such a great friend. If I had no brother and Birgitta was my sister, life would be perfect.

To get to Aleksandra's, I took a route that avoided all of Mama's customers' homes, in case she was delivering garments. Before I could knock on the back door at Aleksandra's, she spotted me through the kitchen window and waved. In seconds she appeared.

"Hello! It is so good to be going out," she chirped in Finnish, seeming heaps happier than when I'd first met her. I had to fight off a sneeze from all the violet talcum she was wearing. She gushed, "You have no idea how much I've been looking forward to this afternoon."

"Me, too. We're off to see 'Mike Donegal's Escape.'" At her confused expression, I added, "That's the name of this week's episode of *The Girl Detective*."

All the way to the Gaiety Theatre, Aleksandra complained about the brats she had to care for. It made me doubt ever wanting to work as a domestic. "But I have good news, too," she said. "The lady of the house is letting me have *every* Wednesday afternoon off."

"Look at the lineup, Aleksandra," I exclaimed. I hoped there would be no one who recognized me and informed my parents.

When we finally neared the head of the line, we realized why it was taking so long. A police officer was enforcing the age restriction. The boy in line ahead of us couldn't have been more than twelve. Before the policeman turned him away, the boy bolted. The officer asked Aleksandra's age, and then we each paid our ten cents and entered the theatre.

"Have you seen a moving picture before?" I asked.

"No, only a Magic Lantern show."

"My father brought me here once. Most of the story is told by the actions, but sometimes there are a few words to read. I can translate them for you."

"Thank you—I can read a little bit of English."

I hid my look of surprise as we took our seats. Mikko didn't think his sister knew much English. How well did brothers really know their older sisters, anyway?

The theatre lights dimmed, hushing the audience, and we were immersed in *The Girl Detective*. The warden at the jail was bamboozled by Mike Donegal's escape. Enter Jean, the Girl Detective. I liked her—she was confident and smart. For some reason she believed Donegal had not left the building. Jean—so brave—began her search of the jail. Everything seemed to be in order.

Suddenly Jean stumbled. We gasped. She had tripped over a man who was bound and gagged. It was likely the work of Donegal. Jean stepped into the furnace room. And there was Donegal!

Aleksandra screamed, clutching my arm.

Then Donegal snatched Jean and knocked her out.

"No!" cried Aleksandra.

Thank goodness the man on the floor had removed his gag by that time and called for help. Men came running. They caught Donegal and rescued Jean. Donegal revealed how he had escaped.

Donegal was a master crook. What if he'd actually escaped? Then a nasty thought hit me. What if Carl Schmidt was a master saboteur? Now that he was on the loose, what if he teamed up with the two men who'd attacked the wireless station? What horrible damage would they cause? I shook my head to rid it of such worries. Surely the police would track them down.

After the show ended, Aleksandra gave me a quick hug. "That was exciting. I didn't think about my job the whole time. Let's come back next Wednesday."

"I know what you mean," I said. "Next Wednesday it is." The only glitch would be if I were hired somewhere, so I added, "Let's meet here in case I'm a little bit late." But getting another job seemed less likely every day.

CHAPTER 24 | John

> "Spain has forbidden its people to discuss the war in public. How we envy Spain!"—The Note Book, *Port Arthur Daily News*, 1915

Papa was already sitting at the kitchen table waiting for supper when I got home. Saara was bent over the sink, draining the boiled potatoes.

"Wash your hands, Jussi," said Mama. "Everything is ready."

I cleaned up and took my place. We dug into our food.

"This morning's newspaper announced more censorship in Canada," said Papa. "Too many military secrets have been leaked to the enemy."

"All over the city ..." I began, with my mouth too full of spuds. I swallowed, then went on, "... folks are talking about nothing but Germans plotting sabotage."

"That's understandable with that German criminal at large," said Papa. "Who knows what trouble he will cause."

"It's sure a good thing soldiers are patrolling more with him on the loose." I broke up my potato with the side of my fork. "Especially at the grain elevators. They're saying once the wheat starts coming, we'll have more than half of Canada's grain stored right here."

"Surely they'll get Carl Schmidt soon," said Saara.

I nibbled on a slice of soft carrot. "I think it's our duty to go to the Anniversary War Service tonight. All of us. Even Saara."

My sister said, "Hrmff" and folded her arms.

She wasn't happy, but I didn't give up trying to convince my parents. "It's a way we can all help the war effort."

Papa agreed it was a fine idea. So did Mama. She even told Saara to leave the dishes and she'd do them herself later. After supper, my whole family was parading to the armoury.

At one point we had to switch to the other side of the street 'cause two loose horses was blocking the sidewalk. Saara wanted to catch them. But Papa said, "Leave them be. That's why Port Arthur hired a pound keeper, to deal with stray animals of all sizes. The lucky man has a job— let him earn his pay."

We joined the crowd jammed into the armoury. After everyone found seats, a choir got us singing hymns. A pastor prayed. He thanked God for our blessings and said, "God in Heaven, we ask for success in this great struggle against the German emperor, Kaiser Wilhelm, and his army."

Then a man stood and read off numbers and names. He didn't have time to read all 1,200 names of Port Arthur men who'd served in the war since it started a year ago. But he did read the names of all the local soldiers who'd died. I got some choked up over one name—Private

Gordon Williams. Richard's brother's dream was to get to France before the war ended, in time to fight. His dream came true. But his fighting was done far too soon.

Reverend Adams spoke in a loud voice and flung his arms about. All of a sudden he grabbed the Canadian Red Ensign flag and waved it high. He shouted, "It's only a rag, this piece of bunting. A glorious old rag, but it's what it stands for! Our red-coated soldiers; our men in khaki; our soldiers in red and blue—they are fighting for this dear old flag! I want it to stand for the blood of our soldiers, the red light of liberty, human liberty. To stand for peace, glorious peace, which will more than compensate us for the men we have lost. Right shall rule! Peace our portion, with Jesus ruling on every hand; may God grant us this."

We all leaped to our feet and clapped hard and long. Then we sang "O Canada" and "God Save the King." Some folks sang different words, about our soldiers in battle instead of King George. They sang, "God save our splendid men; Send them safe home again; God save our men." It was too late for Gordon. I hoped it wasn't too late for the rest of the Port Arthur boys, like Elias and Mr. Entwhistle.

CHAPTER 25 | Saara

"The Kaiser celebrates the war's first anniversary by announcing that he didn't start it."—The Note Book, *Port Arthur Daily News*, 1915

No new want ads! How long could I keep pretending to work at the McLeods'? I was getting weary of all of this acting. I climbed up the hill to my lookout spot. With a sky so packed with grey clouds, Lake Superior looked dull and cold. I shivered, despite the warm temperature.

What was I going to do? Coming up with no answer, I hoofed it down to Birgitta's house to hide out.

Birgitta was starting to make bread. That was a chore I'd perfected. We joked and giggled and still managed to set the bread dough to rise in record time, despite her little sister's "help."

In the middle of cleaning up our mess, there was a loud banging on the door. Birgitta's father slipped on his freshly polished boots and answered the knocking.

"Are you Albert Schmidt?" boomed a male voice.

"Yes," answered Birgitta's father.

"You are under arrest for suspicious behaviour."

Police!

Birgitta's mother cried out in protest and sped to her husband. The rest of us followed.

"Everyone into the parlour while we search the house," ordered the police officer.

"Vati, what are they looking for?" asked Peter, running to grasp his father's arm.

"I do not know. *Komm schnell!*" Mr. Schmidt said, hurrying us into the front room. Birgitta clutched her sister's hand.

I wondered what he'd done that was suspicious. Was he related to Carl Schmidt after all? Was he hiding him? I thought Birgitta had been truthful—what if she had a role in the plots, too? I wanted to flee, but I was too afraid to ask the police officer for permission to leave. Birgitta clung to her mother, quaking, as one constable stood watch and the other two tramped through all the rooms.

Ages later the two men returned carrying letters and German newspapers and books. One looked like a Bible.

"Mr. Schmidt," said the officer in charge, "you are to be interned. Your wife and children can be interned with you, or they will be provided for on government relief."

Families go to internment camps, too?

Mr. Schmidt turned to his wife. "You must stay here and take the relief—"

"No," she said, shaking her head repeatedly. "No … not relief," she croaked, her breath ragged from fear. "I rather be in prison … with you … than pick through garbage of Englishmen to live."

She was choosing internment over her freedom? And

her children's freedom? My breath felt squeezed out of me.

"Then pack your trunk, ma'am," said the officer. "Tonight you, your husband, and your four children will leave for the internment camp."

What did he mean by *four* children? *Oh! He's talking about me!* "Excuse me, sir—I-I'm not their child."

The constable squinted at me. "Who are you, then?"

"Saara Mäki, sir. A friend." My knees were threatening to buckle. He looked skeptical. I added, "I'm a Finlander. I live two houses down."

"Prove it," he said, gripping my arm and pushing me ahead of him. "Is your mother at home?"

"She's a seamstress. She should be there."

He released my arm. Thank goodness, as it already felt bruised. I marched straight to our house, the officer at my side. As I reached for the doorknob, the constable grabbed my arm again and banged on the door. Never was I so relieved to hear Mama's footsteps.

She opened the door and cried out in Finnish, "Saara! What happened?"

"Ma'am, do you speak English?" asked the officer.

"A little."

"What is your name and nationality?"

"Emilia Mäki. I from Finland." Her perplexed eyes searched my face for an explanation. In Finnish she asked, "Are you in trouble?" I shook my head.

"English, please, ma'am," said the constable. "Is this your house?"

"Yes, we rent."

"Who is this girl?"

"She is Saara. My daughter. What happen?"

"I simply needed to confirm her identity. Thank you, ma'am." With that he tipped his cap and strode back toward Birgitta's house.

I flew into Mama's arms, the tears I'd held back now flowing freely. "The police came to Birgitta's house and thought I was her sister. They're sending the entire family away to the 'internment camp,' Mama. How can they do that? They're innocent people."

Mama stroked my hair. "There is much I don't understand. Come inside." She drew me away from the door.

I collapsed onto a kitchen chair, my legs turned to jelly. Mama said nothing as she heated coffee for herself and brewed tea for me.

Mama set our hot drinks on the table and sat opposite me. "Now," she said, "tell me everything. Especially why you were at the Schmidts' house and not at work."

Thud.

That was my heart dropping to my toes. I'd been found out.

Mama listened sympathetically as I explained about my job and the reward money. Then she scolded me for deceiving her and piled on the chores. I guessed she thought I needed to make up for lost time at home.

I scurried to hang the laundry on the clothesline and scrub the floor. While I slogged at the weeding, John hung around smirking at me.

"You missed a bunch of weeds on your left," he chided.

I refused to speak to him.

"I have to make sure you do *this* job right."

Oh, no—how much did Mama tell him? "Leave me alone!" I yelled. "Don't you want to see Peter before he's interned tonight?"

"What! Peter's getting interned?" John looked at me, horrified, then took off at a run.

I wiped my arm across my sweaty forehead. Working as fast as I could, I finally got all the weeds uprooted. I watered the rows, then stowed the tools in the shed.

When I returned to Birgitta's, I found her in her bedroom, distraught, throwing her belongings on her bed.

"Saara, all of this is for a stupid comment Vati made in the job lineup. The men were talking about Carl Schmidt, and Vati said the Nipigon River railway bridge was a good choice of target to sabotage. He did not mean that he would do it, but that the spies were smart." She paced between her bed and dresser. "When he did not get work he left in a huff, and someone told the police. Vati decided to work off steam by walking, and the police followed him." She slammed a pile of German storybooks down next to her collection of German dolls.

About to caution her to be careful of their fragile porcelain heads, I decided not to interrupt. My friend was working off *her* steam by talking.

"Vati is a merchant. He has more schooling than a labourer, but he would never use what or who he knows to spy for Germany. Tell me, what is the crime in walking along the railway tracks? That was his 'suspicious behaviour'! He was not planning to destroy the tracks or a railway bridge or a grain elevator or anything! A simple walk is what our lives are being ruined over! He has obeyed all of the rules about reporting to the registration office as an enemy alien. Oh, I hate those words, *enemy alien*."

I couldn't believe that this was all his charge was based on. I didn't know what to say.

"Mutti told me to pack all of my clothes." Birgitta waved her arm over the bed, saying, "It is not possible to fit everything else in my carpet bag." She lovingly cradled a well-worn doll. Its face looked like real skin. "I will take this one," she said, nestling it in her luggage, "and three books. Will you look after the rest of my dolls and books for me?"

"Of course." I knew better than to ask how long she would be gone. Tears welled in my eyes. "They'll be waiting for you when you come back from Kapuskasing."

"We are not going to Kapuskasing."

"You're not? But the officer said you're going to the internment camp—"

"We are," she said, her red-rimmed eyes boring into mine. "In Vernon—way out in British Columbia! It is the only one that houses German women and children."

When the police came to cart them away, I fiercely hugged Birgitta, both of us crying.

As I carried my friend's treasures home, I wondered what would become of her and her family. Birgitta had promised to write to me, but would I ever hear from her again?

CHAPTER 26 | John

"If the internment camp at Kapuskasing is as fine a place as it is said to be there may be some of us who are not aliens who would like to be."—The Note Book, *Port Arthur Daily News,* 1915

"Hold on a minute," said Fred.

Me and him was on our way back to the *Daily News* building to get more papers on Tuesday morning.

Fred slipped into the bakery and came out with a pastry in each hand. "One newspaper, two sweets," he said, offering one to me.

"Thanks," I said, taking a big bite. "But that trade ain't the fairest deal in the world, pal."

"Is so when you ain't had breakfast yet." He downed the last bit of his pastry and licked his fingers. "Wish I had another paper—I'd do it again."

"How come you didn't grab something to eat at home?"

"Nothing in the cupboard or the icebox." He shrugged, as if it wasn't the first time. "But relief money should be handed out today. Then we can buy groceries."

I chewed this over as we crossed Pearl Street.

"You know," he said, "sometimes I think me and my mother should've got interned with my father."

"Fred, that's crazy."

"He says the food ain't great, but he gets three meals every day. Could be that Peter's better off than me."

"You're talking like a fool—Peter's a prisoner!" It was five days since he'd left. Every time I thought of him stuck in the internment camp, it felt like someone slugged me in the stomach. "He can't go anywhere and he ain't got his friends."

"Maybe he's got new friends there."

"Living here you get to go to school and—"

"There I wouldn't *have* to go to school and I'd like that."

"Here you get to live in your own house."

"Without my father." He sounded so glum.

"And here you can earn money."

"Sure, but not enough to help much."

That sparked an idea in my noggin. Fred had been a newsboy longer than me, but he never earned as much as I did in a week. "Say, pal, what do you think of sharing my paper route? I kind of miss having more time to hawk papers." A grin began growing on Fred's face. "If you did my route on Tuesday, Thursday, and Saturday, I could keep my favourite corner longer those days. What do you say?"

"That sounds like the fairest deal in the world," he said. "So, can I start now? It's Tuesday."

"Why not?"

Fred took off like a stone fired from a slingshot.

At home that evening, I hunched over my scrapbook at the table. I was pasting in another newspaper clipping.

Saara showed up to get a drink of water before going to bed.

"They found German spies dressed as women on a steamship," I said.

"Is this a joke?"

"No, listen." I read:

Three German submarines chased the Pretoria *after it left Scotland heading to North America. The steamship finally evaded the submarines. Not long after, the wireless operator on board discovered three German spies disguised as women trying to send wireless messages to the submarines. The* Pretoria's *officers wasted no time arresting the spies.*

I looked up at Saara. "What if there are German spies disguised as women right here in Port Arthur? Think what damage they could cause with no one suspecting a thing."

She thought for a moment. Then her hand flew up to her mouth and her eyes opened wide. "I wonder if that's what happened to Mama's dress that went missing."

CHAPTER 27 | Saara

"The won't-works should be mobilized throughout the Dominion. With the greatest crop in the history of the West waiting to be harvested, no longer can it be pleaded that there is nothing for them to do."
—*Port Arthur Daily News*, 1915

The next morning, I wondered aloud to Mama how Birgitta and her family were doing. I punched the bread dough I was kneading. "It's so unfair to send people away."

She banged the lid back into its hole in the wood stove. "There is no more room in this country for sympathy toward Germans. Toward any foreigners, it seems. Be extremely careful what you say in public, Saara. I can't afford to lose any more customers or have anyone think we are disloyal."

I decided to say nothing and kept kneading.

"*Voi, voi,*" said Mama, rummaging in the cupboard. "We say in the Old Country, 'Happiness is a place between too much and too little.' I'm worried that we're getting too close to too little."

I covered the dough with a clean tea towel, then picked up the newspaper and turned to the classified section.

I remembered seeing a daily ad that might interest a skilled seamstress like Mama. *Found it.*

"Here's a way you can make money," I said, pointing to the ad. "The Auto Knitted Hosiery Company in Toronto says ladies can earn ten dollars or more a week working from home on Auto Knitting machines. Would you like me to write them a letter for you?"

"Only if you use my real name," she said in a no-nonsense tone, but with a wink.

Blushing at the reminder of "Sarah McKee," I picked up Sipu and buried my warm face in her fur. She felt different. "Does Sipu look bigger to you?"

"Pass her to me," said Mama. Sitting with Sipu on her lap, she gingerly felt my cat's belly. "I'd say Sipu's going to be a mother."

"How soon?"

"At least a month, maybe longer. But we can't afford more than one cat. You'll have to find homes for the kittens."

It was hard to feel excited about Sipu's litter. Even my kittens were going to be sent away.

I raced through the rest of my kitchen chores and left for the garden. I wanted to finish working there before going to the show with Aleksandra. Then my conscience pronged me. How could I spend money on seeing a moving picture when Mama was so worried? I decided I had to keep my promise to Aleksandra, but I wouldn't go to any more shows after this.

Halfway through weeding a row, my heart lurched at the thought of Birgitta in British Columbia. How long would she be there? It was hard to believe her family had been sent so far away. Were they getting enough to eat? How would Birgitta spend her time in the internment camp? I surprised myself by how much I ached missing her.

Now Helena treated me as if I didn't exist. A tear slid down my cheek. I wasn't just sad; I roiled with anger. We'd been friends for eight years. Didn't she know me well enough to trust my judgment of Birgitta? I felt desperate for time with a friend. Clouds settled in, keeping the temperature cool, helping me work quickly.

By the time I returned the gardening tools to the shed, there was a light drizzle. How fortunate—no need to water. At home I changed into a clean dress and set off to meet Aleksandra at the Gaiety Theatre.

She wasn't out front. The show was about to start, so she must have purchased her ticket already. It was hard work convincing the attendant of this. But he finally sold me a ticket, saying, "If the cop was here, I wouldn't do this." I found Aleksandra inside, in the same row as before.

"Hello, Saara," said Aleksandra in a cheery voice. "It's *The Girl Detective* again. I know I'll like it."

The lights dimmed and the moving picture began. This episode, "The Clairvoyant Swindlers," featured a different girl detective, called Bertha. At the first sight of Rillando, the clairvoyant, I thought of the palmist in the tent telling Birgitta's future. *You have a long journey ahead*, she had predicted. The palmist had got the long journey part right, only it was in the opposite direction from what

Birgitta had hoped, and certainly not the circumstances she'd imagined. The fortune teller had also said Birgitta had a strong, loving family, but there was no happiness. Had she only said that out of spite once she learned Birgitta was German? I prayed my friend's loving family would stay strong through whatever lay ahead for them.

When the show ended, Aleksandra said, "See you here next Wednesday?"

"I'd like to, but I can't afford the ticket."

"I'd be happy to pay for yours," she said as we stepped outside. "A thank you for getting me coming here."

"Could you wait for me out here, even if it's raining?" I asked. "I almost wasn't let in today without an older person with me."

"Mikko just turned fifteen, so he's old enough to bring you, too," said Aleksandra with a grin. "If only he had more time when he comes to town."

I blushed so intensely I was sure even my hair part was red.

As we passed a tailor's shop, the stocky young man loitering in the doorway waved at Aleksandra and winked.

I whispered, "Do you know him?"

"No." It was Aleksandra's turn to blush.

He trotted after us, catching up as we reached the Rexall store. "Hello, ladies. May I interest you in some chocolate creams and nougatines? They have a tasty selection in here," he said, pointing to the drugstore.

He seemed pleasant enough, with perfect English, yet he was a stranger. Aleksandra stood at least two inches taller than him. I tugged at her sleeve to keep her walking, but she decided to stop.

"Yes, please," she said to him, as if English were her first language. As they turned into the store, I rolled my eyes at their backs. It was time for me to go home.

Along the way, I made a point of saying a loud hello to Mr. Campbell. He ignored me, so I raised my voice even more, in case his hearing had worsened. He grumbled something under his breath. "Pardon me, what did you say?" I asked.

"I don't want to talk to you," he said without looking at me.

"Why not?"

Then he faced me. "I've seen you chumming with that German girl, and I know what happened to her family. I have no time for German-lovers."

"But Birgitta's father is innocent—"

"How do you know for sure?"

How *did* I know? I only had Birgitta's word. I remembered the doubt I'd felt myself when the police had come to search the house.

"That silence of yours tells me you don't. Pardon me, but I have patriotic work to do," he said, bending to pull weeds.

CHAPTER 28 | John

"Port Arthur and Fort William will handle more grain this year than in the period that gave them second place among the grain ports of the continent. In the language of 1912 we're whooptimistic."—The Note Book, *Port Arthur Daily News*, 1915

I was first to hoist my sheaf of papers and head off. Today's pitch was easy: *CARL SCHMIDT LOCKED UP AGAIN!*

Fred was going to hawk papers, too, then do my route. It felt good to know he'd bring home some extra money for his family. Even if I sold another sheaf, I'd be done before him and have nothing to do.

Before I reached the end of the lane, Cam's motorcar turned in. He slowed when he spotted me.

"Hey, Scoop!" he called. "Want to come to police court with me this morning?"

"Yes, sir!"

"Meet me back here in one hour," said Cam. He waved and drove on.

This is bully! I hawked a load of newspapers. Then I headed back to wait for Cam.

Only minutes after I returned to the *Daily News* building, he drove up. "Hop in."

I climbed aboard and we roared away.

When we reached the police court, Cam pointed to the back seat of his motorcar. "You'll find a notebook and pencil behind me. Get reporting, Scoop."

"Yes, sir!"

"Drop the *sir*, okay? I'm not your boss or anything."

"Okay, Cam!"

We found two seats together. Cam pulled out his own notebook. *Whew.* I was keen to try getting everything down on paper, but I wasn't sure I could keep up. The first item was underway. I began scribble-printing, putting in question marks where I missed something or planned to check with Cam later.

> *Douglas Winters drunk last night. Going home he made disterbinse in streetcar. Fined $5 and ?*
>
> *CPR police chief says wheat stealing started again in railway yards. Warning thieves makes no diffrence. They make good money—sell wheat for $1 a bag. Two forenners (women) arrested—put on suspended sentence?*

A police officer hauled a scruffy man in front of the magistrate. I scrambled to get all of the details written down.

> *Austrian man (name?) sent to jail for 3 months for stealing clothes from clotheslines in Port Arthur. Landlady at his bording house turned him in to police when he wanted to pay his bill with stolen goods.*

181

Court room table heaped with clothes, pillow slips, sheets.

Police court was over for today. I sat back and shook the cramp out of my right hand.

Cam smiled. "How'd you do, Scoop?"

I showed Cam my notebook and glanced at his. He'd filled in two pages with tiny handwriting. My printed lines took up only one page.

Cam patted my shoulder. "A fine start. You'll get more details down with practice."

"Did you know I want to be a reporter?"

He chuckled. "Oh, I figured as much."

"What do they do with stolen goods, like the clothes up there?" I pointed to the table. "Do they return them to the owners?"

"Why, did something go missing from your clothesline?"

"My mother's dress."

"Could you identify it?"

"I think so."

"Let's go ask."

We made our way over to the table. A man was piling the sheets into a crate.

"The lad here might know who owns some of these clothes," said Cam.

"Have a look," said the man, "but be quick."

I hunted through the stack of shirts and dresses. "Aha!" I recognized a familiar green dress. I held it up. "This is my mother's."

"Go ahead and take it. One less thing for me to deal with."

I rolled the dress and tucked it under my arm, grinning. "Is Mama ever going to be surprised."

CHAPTER 29 | Saara

"The Fifty-Second Band is drumming up recruits. You can't beat the band."—The Note Book, *Port Arthur Daily News*, 1915

I started rushing to answer a knock on our door Monday afternoon, but John must have already been on his way out.

"Helena!" he exclaimed. "Haven't seen you around here all summer."

"Is your sister home?" she asked.

"Yup." He started hollering my name, but I was already behind him.

"Hello, Saara," said Helena. She hugged me, then stepped back. "I thought that since you-know-who has left," she said, glancing sideways at Birgitta's empty house, "we could go roller skating."

"Uh … okay."

"Great," said Helena, grinning.

The letter carrier arrived. Even though my brother and I were standing right there, Helena reached out her hand for our mail—one letter.

Helena studied the envelope, then thrust it at me, glaring. "For you."

A familiar name was printed in the upper left corner. "My first letter from Birgitta!" I danced a jig. Forgetting I had an audience, I began ripping open the envelope.

Helena exhaled sharply. "That you can carry on being *friends* with a despicable German is incomprehensible."

I stopped and gaped at her. "Not *all* Germans are despicable," I said, my voice shaking with fury.

Helena stormed away.

"Does this mean you ain't going roller skating?" said John.

Still fuming at Helena's prejudice, I shoved him aside. "Move!" I snapped and headed back inside to read the letter from my *real* friend.

Birgitta had been gone a week and a half. She must have posted this as soon as she arrived at the internment camp.

Miss Birgitta Schmidt
Vernon, B.C., Canada, Internment Camp,
August 5th, 1915

Dear Saara,
The train has only just started to move and I am
writing to you as I promised. We must travel the

entire way under guard! They sent a constable with
us to make sure we do not try to escape. Peter thinks
this is the most wonderful adventure. He chats with
the constable and everyone who passes by. He found
out we will not reach the mountains for three whole
days! I plan to sleep.

We were in such a rush before leaving that Mutti
forgot about the tins of fish and canned fruit left in
our house. She wanted you to take them. Now she is
asking if you could please tell Mr. Campbell about the
food (and while you are there, give Tiger a pat for
me). Maybe the food will help him rent out the house.

I remembered my last conversation with Mr.
Campbell. Mr. Schmidt had been right about why their
rent was raised—Mr. Campbell didn't want German
people in the house he now owned. No, I would pat
Tiger, but I would not tell Mr. Campbell about the food
left behind. He could find out for himself. I returned to
reading Birgitta's letter.

It is Friday now. There is nothing to see except flat
land and fields of wheat. I am going back to sleep.
Now we are almost at the mountains. I can see them
in the distance. Saara, you must believe me that my
father did nothing wrong. What he said about the
bridge was innocent. He would never cause Canada
harm. I hold no hope of convincing the authorities,
though. They are determined not to listen.

I had such a fright just now! The train climbed

higher, then all of a sudden it got dark. My ears told me the train was still rolling along the track, but my fear told me we were falling into a gorge. My heart nearly jumped out the window. Back in the sunlight, I realized we had gone through a tunnel. Well, it was only the first. They were the Spiral Tunnels. Can you imagine a train travelling in circles?

We changed to a different train in Sicamous, British Columbia, that took us to Vernon. There the constable loaded us in a patrol wagon to get to the internment camp. It is a dried out, dusty piece of level land surrounded by barbed wire with no lake or creek in sight. I do not think much of our new "home." Vati and Mutti were each given a P.O.W. number—that means <u>Prisoner</u> of War! Then they had to hand over their money and jewellery. I wonder if they will ever see their valuables again.

I am anxiously waiting to receive a letter from you, Saara. Please do not keep me waiting for long.

Your loving friend,
Birgitta

Prisoner of War! How horrible to be called that. And to be stuck in that waterless spot! All my life I'd lived next to huge Lake Superior, free to explore green forests. I pictured Birgitta in such a dry, flat place, and a lump swelled in my throat—I knew I'd hate to live there. I pulled out paper and pencil and wrote back to her immediately. But before I got it in the mail the next morning, another letter arrived from her.

Miss Birgitta Schmidt
Vernon, B.C., Canada, Internment Camp,
August 9th, 1915

Dear Saara,
I cannot wait to receive a letter from you before
writing again. Saara, you are like a sister and it
hurts to not see you anymore.
There are several German families here. Also,
there are many Austro-Hungarian men (the guards
call them Austrians, but most of them call themselves
Ukrainians). Some high-class Germans from
Vancouver are here—even a Baron, a Countess,
and a doctor. They live in the first-class section of the
camp. We live in the second-class married quarters,
next to the second-class area for just men. My family
is treated better than the men in second-class. We
have our own fairly comfortable cabin (it is a small,
black tar-papered hut with a canvas roof). I say
"fairly" because of the summer heat. Vernon feels
like an oven, day and night! I dare not go outdoors
without the straw hat they gave me. I also needed
a kerchief over my mouth and nose today—the hot
wind stirred up the dust.

We are guarded day and night by soldiers from the nearby military camp. Today a bugler led a new group of about 30 marching here to trade places with the old group. Last night I hardly slept and not only because of the heat. I heard the sentries shout from their posts every half hour or more!

My parents are worried over a rumour spreading around the camp, that we could be sent to Germany. I cannot wait until this nightmare is over and I can return to Port Arthur.

Your loving friend,
Birgitta

I was horrified—surely Canada wouldn't send them back to Germany! I added reassurances to my letter and hurried to post it before Birgitta's next letter could arrive.

CHAPTER 30 | John

"To the boys of the Fifty-Second, God speed and
a safe return."—The Note Book, *Port Arthur Daily
News*, 1915

Saara was trudging up the back lane ahead of me.

"Wait up," I called.

She didn't even turn around. Instead she started walking faster. I ran to catch up.

"Listen," I said, panting. "I thought we was safe when
they sent Carl Schmidt and Gustav Stephen to the internment camp last week. But every day there's more in the
papers about German plots to destroy places. Ammunition factories, railway bridges, ships."

"Those are only in the U.S., not in Canada anymore,"
she scoffed.

"But look at this," I said, holding out the newspaper.
"I'm worried there're more German spies right here."

That got her attention. She began reading aloud, "As
a patriotic citizen I deem it my duty to inform you and the
people of Canada that a gigantic plot is on foot among
aliens of German and Austrian birth to destroy the twin
ports' wonderful system of grain elevators."

I blurted, "It says they ain't gonna blow 'em up but bring in rats to eat the grain or ruin it. How's the militia going to fight rats?"

"John, listen," she said, laughing. "This is no threat."

"Saara, this is for real."

"What's real is the cool weather that's coming to-night." We'd reached the Entwhistles' backyard and she turned in. "I need to cover the cucumbers." Handing back the paper, she said, "This 'plot' is part of The Note Book—the editor is simply playing a joke."

I didn't give up. "Saara, I'm not making all this up. Look!" I demanded, shoving the *Daily News* front page at her. She stopped clearing the table for supper. *"ALLEGED GERMAN SPY IS TAKEN FROM TRAIN AT SCHREIBER,"* I read. I couldn't keep my voice from trembling. "He almost made it to Port Arthur."

Sighing, she said, "Tell me what *alleged* means."

"Something legal-like I think," I said.

"It means possible, not for sure, NO PROOF, John. Don't be foolish. Any spies who were here earlier this summer are long gone."

"But I bet there's a German plot to blow up the grain elevators! They're saying it's the best wheat crop *ever*. It won't be long before trains of grain cars start coming into Port Arthur." Each of my sentences came out faster than the one before. "The grain has to feed the troops and horses and the whole empire! If-the-Germans-destroy-it-what-are-we-going-to-do?"

"Quit it right now! I don't want to hear *one more thing*

from you about spies and plots, okay? Just forget about all of this."

"That's *enough*, you two," said Mama, poking a knife in the potatoes boiling on the wood stove. "Or do I need to pull out the switch?"

Both me and Saara had sharp memories of the switch's sting on the back of our legs. We stopped our bickering. I thought I was grown past the need for the switch. But I guessed Mama didn't agree. And now likely wasn't the best time to try to change her mind.

"Another few minutes and we can eat," said Mama. "Finish clearing the table, Saara."

My sister stacked my library books to move them to the parlour. *All About Rifles and Ammunition. All About Railways. All About Engineering. All About Airships.* She muttered, "Oh, give me a *story* any day."

In the dark of night, I heard a bang. I jumped out of bed, ran into the hallway, and collided with Saara coming out of the bathroom. "Did you hear the explosion? I saw the flash, too. Sure wish we had a telephone so's I could call the police."

She snarled at me. "Arrrg—it was only thunder and lightning. Stop being such a scaredy-cat. Don't bother me anymore with your jokes and nonsense about spies. Go back to bed."

Why wouldn't she believe me? I knew lots of jokes— the grain plot wasn't one of them.

The next day I met Saara in the porch when she returned from doing all the gardening.

"A letter came for you this morning," I said, "from Mr. Graham."

"Finally!" she said. Saara charged into the house with me right behind. "I've been watching for it every day." She checked the kitchen table. But all she found was another letter from Birgitta. "Where's Mr. Graham's letter?"

"Oh, I think it got tossed in the wood stove by accident." I struggled to keep a straight face, then burst out laughing. "There was no letter from him, silly."

"What?"

"Now, *that's* a joke."

"No, that's cruel. Beyond cruel!" she said, giving me a firm shove. "Grow up!"

CHAPTER 31 | Saara

"It is said that there is a possibility of the standard of height of recruits being lowered to five feet one inch. Why not? The stocky man deserves his chance. Napoleon was a runt."—The Note Book, *Port Arthur Daily News*, 1915

Birgitta had written her third letter the day after her last one.

Miss Birgitta Schmidt
Vernon, B.C., Canada, Internment Camp,
August 10th, 1915

Dear Saara,
My letters to you are my journal so you must keep them for me. After we finished our chores today (yes, we all have to look after our huts and cook for ourselves), Peter and I explored every square inch of our PRISON. Besides the rows of huts with their

little flower gardens, there is a large vegetable garden and tennis court. The friendly sentry told us it was turned into a skating rink last winter. He said the big building here used to be a jail. Then it was turned into a Hospital for the Insane. Depending on how long we are imprisoned here, this <u>whole camp</u> could become a Home for the Insane. Everyone is worried not knowing how long we must stay here or what will happen to us when we are finally let out.

Back to the tour of my new home. All around this property stands the barbed wire fence that keeps us penned ███████████████████████████
███████████████████████████
███████████████████████████
█████████████████ *and stare at the brown hills dotted with trees. I will stop here—the Young Men's Christian Association workers have arrived to teach English classes. I never thought I would call learning a language fun.*

Your loving friend,
Birgitta

Why had Birgitta crossed out those lines? Why so heavily that I couldn't see any of the words? Then I saw the "Passed by Internment Censor" stamp at the top of the page. *Of course.* It was the censor who had blackened the words that weren't allowed. Now I was extra curious to know what Birgitta had written. But no matter how much light shone behind the paper, I couldn't make out a single consonant or vowel in the blackened section.

After lunch, Mama headed back to her work and I washed our dishes in record time.

"Where're you rushing off to?" asked John.

"I'm going to see a moving picture with Mikko's sister."

"Lucky you. I've never seen one," he whined. "Can I come with you?"

"No." Hearing that annoying whine and remembering his behaviour on the streetcar made me certain I didn't want him tagging along. "Find someone else to take you."

"Like who? Papa and Mama won't," he groused, sounding hurt.

I set off to the Gaiety Theatre. Aleksandra met me outside as usual, but she was not alone. At her side with an ear-to-ear grin was Mr. Nougatine. It turned out his name was Jim and he was keen to join us. He even paid for all of our tickets. I was surprised when Aleksandra and Jim sat with me instead of finding seats in the back row. *Should I write to Mikko about Jim?* I was sure he'd want to know about him.

"Scotty Weed's Alibi" began to play on the screen. I was pleased to see the girl detective Jean again. I preferred her over Bertha. Jean was investigating the theft of a diamond tiara. As much as I had wanted to come, my mind was barely on the show. School was starting in two weeks, and I *still* hadn't heard anything from Mr. Graham. What if I had to repeat Junior Fourth? My arms turned to gooseflesh. I would not become a teacher. My dream would be finished.

Scotty Weed was trying to establish his alibi. Would he find a witness? He had to prove he was somewhere other than the scene of the crime when the tiara was stolen. I tried hard to focus on the story, but my thoughts wandered away again. What would this next school year be like with Birgitta away and Helena not speaking to me? If she wasn't glaring at me, she'd be preoccupied with Richard. And now Aleksandra had a beau. By the time the show was over, I'd imagined myself as best friends with every remaining girl in my class in turn. I didn't like any of the possibilities.

"Will you come next Wednesday, Saara?" asked Aleksandra. "My treat."

"No," I said, "but thank you." It was too awkward coming with the two of them. Besides, although Jim tried to hide it, I could tell he was pleased when I said no. "Goodbye."

On my way home, a livery horse caught my eye. He was small but hauling an overloaded wagon with ease. *Canuck!* He was a Canadian horse—Mikko's favourite breed. The little horse amazed me with his strength and pluck. The Remount Purchaser had overlooked Canuck because of his size, but I figured he could outpull and outlast most of the horses recruited for the war. Still, I was glad for Canuck's sake he'd been left behind.

Monday brought another letter from Birgitta. I anxiously opened the envelope, hoping it wasn't full of horrible news.

Miss Birgitta Schmidt
Vernon, B.C., Canada, Internment Camp,
August 13, 1915

Dear Saara,
I was so busy yesterday (the 12th) I missed writing to
you! The Y.M.C.A. workers said my English is very
good. They asked me to teach the younger children so
they could teach the adults. There are lots of children
here. I am the oldest. As well as having me teach
English, the parents also ask me to look after the little
ones so they can get their "work" done. I believe the
women actually work—but I have seen too many men
playing poker to think that is not part of the reason.
One man is too sick to even play card games. He coughs
all the time and though he is eating, he gets thinner.

That sounded like Auntie when she was fighting tuberculosis. I made a mental note to warn Birgitta to stay away from him or she could catch it, too.

███████████████████████████████

███████████████████████████████

███████████████████████

Mutti wants to know if you told Mr. Campbell
about the food we left in our house.

No, I hadn't, and I wasn't planning to talk to him ever again.

Now it is the 14th. I am still waiting for a letter from you. Please take a few minutes to tell me your news. I will not be able to write to you as often. The friendly sentry warned me that I send too many letters—it looks suspicious. He said ▓▓▓▓▓▓▓▓▓▓
▓▓▓▓▓▓▓▓▓▓▓▓▓▓▓▓▓▓▓▓▓▓▓▓
▓▓▓▓▓▓▓▓▓▓▓▓▓▓▓▓▓▓▓▓▓▓▓▓
▓▓▓▓▓▓▓▓▓▓

August 16th. Peter! I could wring his neck! A soldier told us rattlesnakes live here in the Okanagan Valley, then Peter said he found one in the privy. I did not go there all day. When I could not wait any longer, I asked Vati to check for snakes and he said no. I heard Peter snickering. He made it up! I was so mad I almost wet myself. That would have been embarrassing. You are not alone with brother troubles!

Your loving friend who is desperate for a letter,
Birgitta

Brothers! What pains they could be. Surely my first letter would have reached her by now. Unless they would censor my writing, too. Most likely they would, and that could explain the delay. Alarmed, I thought through my quite personal letter. I hadn't written anything suspicious, had I?

CHAPTER 32 | John

"Von Bernstorff, the German ambassador at
Washington, is only that in name. He's a spy."
—The Note Book, *Port Arthur Daily News*, 1915

We was finishing Sunday supper when Mama said to my
sister, "You look upset. What's bothering you?"

"School starts in three days and I still haven't heard
Mr. Graham's decision. I don't know whether I can go into
Senior Fourth."

I kept quiet, thinking hard. So *that* was why she was all
worked up about getting a letter from the principal. She
was scared she'd have to redo Junior Fourth. This would've
never happened if she hadn't missed school—she was far
too smart.

Saara began gathering the dishes for washing. Mama
and Papa settled in the parlour, but I stayed behind in the
kitchen.

Staring at the table, I took a giant breath. Then I blew
out and said, "Remember when I told you a letter came
from Mr. Graham?"

"How could I forget? I can't ever trust you. How could
you pull a prank about something so important to me?"

"I never understood till now why it mattered so much to you." Her eyes looked full of hurt. "It was a dumb thing to do. And mean. I'm sorry."

She glared my way like she wanted to strangle me. Then she said, "Even meaner was hiding my scribbler in the first place."

I sprang to my feet and shoved my chair hard against the table. "I told you before, I didn't do *anything* with your scribbler!" I yelled. "I never *touched* your scribbler!"

"What's going on in here?" asked Papa from the doorway.

Saara explained about her scribbler going missing in July and how she might have to repeat her school year.

"Was that the notebook where you wrote about helping Arvo and Marja at the farm?"

"Yes. And there were mathematics equations and a graph."

Papa nodded.

Saara looked stunned. "How do you know about it?"

"I saw the notebook on the table one morning and read it while I ate breakfast. Your writing has improved."

"Thank you."

I could tell she was puzzling out what had happened. Me, too.

Saara asked, "What did you do with my scribbler after you finished reading?"

"That was too long ago—I don't remember. I must have been up early that day, because I had time to read my Finnish newspaper, too."

Oh! Now I can prove it wasn't my fault! "I know what

he did with it!" I exclaimed. "When Papa's done with his Finnish papers, he tosses them in the woodbox. Your scribbler must have gotten mixed in with his newspaper that day. See? I said you can trust me." I headed to the stairs.

"John, I'm sorry," said Saara. "I should have believed you."

It sounded like she meant it. But I just shook my head and kept walking away.

CHAPTER 33 | Saara

"During the next three months it will be just as
necessary to recruit men for the harvest fields as to
recruit them for active service."—The Note Book,
Port Arthur Daily News, 1915

On Monday morning, another familiar envelope arrived.

Passed by Interument Censor
AUG 24 1915
Vernon, B.C.

Miss Birgitta Schmidt
Vernon, B.C., Canada, Internment Camp,
August 23rd, 1915

Dear Saara,
Your letter came today! Thank you, thank you, thank
you! If you received all of my letters so far, you already
have the answers to your questions. That is the problem
with such distance. Never mind. Who cares if we repeat
ourselves. Knowing that you miss me, too, and pray for
us, makes this prison more bearable.

*Believe it or not, I am so happy I even hugged Peter.
Not just because of your letter, but something wonderful
happened. Before one of the ladies was sent here, she had
been pregnant almost a dozen times, but all the babies
were born dead. She had given up hope of ever having
a child to raise. Another baby was on the way. The camp
doctor treated her with a new medicine and this time
her baby lived! Every one of the prisoners (and even
most of the soldiers!) crowded around the main gate to
welcome them back from the hospital yesterday.*

*With the camp in such high spirits, the Y.M.C.A.
singsong last night was the best (and loudest) so far.
The drama usually gets only a few chuckles, but not this
time. The actors hardly said or did anything funny and
the crowd all laughed. After, some people got out their
instruments and gave a concert. I did not want the
happy day to end. But then your letter came today and
now my happiness can last a while longer.*

Your loving friend,
Birgitta

In the afternoon, I parked on the steps out front with a
library book, waiting for the letter carrier. Soon I reached
the point in the story where I didn't want to stop until
the end.

"Hall-o, miss," called the letter carrier, startling me.
"Are you keeping watch so your wee kitty doesn't climb
the tree?"

"No, I—"

He chuckled. "Here's your mail, miss."

"Thank you," I said, closing my book and reaching for the stack of envelopes.

My heart skipped a beat or two. On top was a letter from Mr. Graham! "Thank you so much!"

"You are welcome, miss," he said, waving farewell as he continued on his route.

At last I would learn my results. Tearing open the envelope, I unfolded the single piece of paper and read Mr. Graham's precise handwriting.

Dear Miss Mäki,
I have completed my review of your individualized school assignments. While I find the work satisfactory overall and your composition skills exemplary, my superiors have informed me that I must abide by school policy.

My hope-bubble burst. I felt like I was listing, as if on a sinking ship. He was going to keep me back in Junior Fourth. I forced the thought away and kept reading.

I will give you a promotion on approval with two months' trial in Senior Fourth. On the first of November, I shall review your progress and make a final decision. If you make good, you will continue with the class, but if you are not meeting the requirements, you will be returned to the lower grade.
Yours truly,
Mr. R. Graham, Principal

I got a trial promotion! I didn't have to repeat! Cheering, I jumped up and down a few times. "Thank you, Mr. Graham," I said, grinning. Then I ran upstairs to tell Mama my good news.

By November 1 Mr. Graham would realize I belonged in Senior Fourth. He'd know my performance well—he was the Senior Fourth teacher.

I stopped at Helena's back gate out of habit but then kept walking. It was the first day of school. Oh, how I longed for a friend in my class. When the bell rang, I made my way to the Senior Fourth classroom.

Helena and Richard were already seated, deep in conversation. They didn't look up as I slipped into a seat a couple of rows away. By the time Mr. Graham appeared and began taking attendance, a third of the desks were still empty. Many families had moved away since June. Fathers were searching for work in other Canadian cities. Birgitta's house still stood vacant wearing its For Rent sign in the front window.

We sang "God Save the King," and Mr. Graham read the Scripture. Then we lined up to collect our school supplies. Unintentionally, I wound up behind Richard. I whispered, "Good morning."

He turned his head and said, "Good—" Then Helena grabbed his arm and pulled him forward. This was worse than I'd imagined it would be.

As I carefully balanced my scribblers, foolscap, drawing book, box of drawing crayons, blotter, pen points and holders, ruler, and pencils, I avoided looking in their direction. I desperately prayed for a new friend.

At the end of the day, after singing "The Maple Leaf Forever," we were finally dismissed. I hurried to the door, but Mr. Graham called me over to his desk.

"Due to your presence in my classroom, I assume you received my letter?" he asked.

"Yes, sir."

"Do you understand that you are on trial until November?"

"Yes, and then you'll decide whether I can continue." I squared my shoulders. "You won't be disappointed, sir. I'll work hard and meet all of your requirements."

CHAPTER 34 | John

"Enlist today! No man of military age and without
dependents now has good reason for failure to enlist."
—The Note Book, *Port Arthur Daily News*, 1915

Papa stormed through the porch and into the kitchen,
where I was pasting clippings in my scrapbook. I was getting behind after only two days of school.

"I need coffee," he said, scowling. He grabbed a cup,
and Saara filled it from the pot on the wood stove. "Emilia!"
he bellowed.

"I'm coming," called Mama from upstairs.

The grain elevators had started hiring. Papa'd gone to
the one at the foot of Bay Street to see about part-time
work. I guessed it hadn't gone well.

"What happened?" asked Mama. I didn't like how
worried she sounded.

"They will only hire Canadian-born and British sub-
jects. Can you believe it? I'm a hard worker and they won't
even give me a chance." He slurped his coffee. "Then all I
did was bang the door on the way out, and the soldier on
guard pulled me aside to question me. Had to repeat the
whole thing to him."

He was still riled up. He probably did more than simply slam the door.

"Tauno," said Mama, placing her hand on his shoulder, "go lie down until supper's ready."

A while later there was a loud knock on our door. I found two policemen standing outside. They didn't look friendly.

The heavyset officer said, "We need to talk to Mr. Tauno Mäki. Is he home?"

He didn't say Papa's name right, but I knew that's who they wanted. But why? My heart was thump-thumping. "Yes, I'll get him. Come in." I led them into the parlour and dashed upstairs.

"Papa, wake up," I said, shaking his shoulder. "The police are here."

Groggy from his nap, Papa mumbled, "What?" and got to his feet. His hair was sticking up on the sides.

"The police want to see you." I followed him down the stairs. Now my stomach was curdling.

"Are you Tauno Mäki?" asked the burly officer, while the shorter policeman pulled out a notebook and pencil.

"Yes. What is this about?"

"We have a few questions for you. Take a seat." The officers stayed standing.

Mama and Saara joined us. Both of their faces had gone pale. The policeman grilled Papa about what happened at the grain elevator.

"What is your nationality?"

"Finnish."

The officer raised his dark eyebrows, saying, "How do

we know you aren't an enemy alien passing yourself off as a Finlander? Show us your identity papers."

Why did he doubt Papa's word?

The policeman studied Papa's papers. He handed them back, saying, "Thank you. These confirm your identity. Now, is it true you are attempting to organize a union?"

"Yes—it is the only way to improve the workers' lot," said my father. He explained his activities in clear English. I felt proud, hearing he was so determined to make working conditions better.

When the policemen was done, we walked with them to the porch. In a hushed tone, the note-taking officer told Papa, "Back off the union work."

Papa closed the door after them.

"Tauno, you should stop going to labour meetings," said Mama. She folded her arms tightly across her chest as if she was cold.

"Why should I?" he replied. "I'm doing nothing illegal. How else will workers be treated fairly?"

Early on Friday morning, me and Fred was shooting marbles behind the *Daily News* building when Ricky stormed up. He grabbed my shirt front.

"Word's gotten around yer gettin' favours from Mr. Cameron," he growled, shoving me against the brick wall. "That's how you got your paper route, ain't it?" Ricky was at least a head taller than me. He'd been griping all summer about not having his own route.

"No, I—"

"Leave him alone, Ricky," said Fred, trying to pull him off me.

Instead, one of Ricky's pals yanked Fred away and threw him to the ground.

"Hun-lovers don't deserve any favours," snarled Ricky. In a flash, I was eating dirt beside Fred. It felt like ten boots kicking my sides all at once. "You stop being a toady to Mr. Cameron, or I'll beat you to a pulp."

"Hey, boys, break it up!" called Joe. "Papers are ready."

"Dirty Finlander," hissed Ricky. He kicked my foot as he left.

Fred gave me a hand up. I winced as I straightened. I whacked my clothes to knock off some of the dirt. My finger caught in a tear by one of my buttons and ripped my shirt farther.

"Your mother ain't going to be happy 'bout that," said Fred.

That wasn't the worst of it. Ricky took off with his sheaf of papers, and I knew where he was headed: my high-selling corner. There was no point trying to fight him for it, so I picked a different spot. Careful to hold a paper so it hid my torn shirt, I shouted my pitch. What I would've rather bellowed was *"UGLY SCRAP! NEWSBOY WANTS REVENGE!"*

After I sold out, I did my route. Now I had to skedaddle home and change so's I could get to school on time. Saara's nasty wish for me had partly come true—I was in the dreaded Miss Pritchard's class. She hadn't been hard on me in the first two days and I didn't want to give her any reason to start.

I sneaked into the house. My heart sank when I found Mama and Saara still at the kitchen table.

"Oh, Jussi, look at you!" said Mama, staring at my torn shirt.

"What happened?" asked Saara.

"Sorry about the rip, Mama," I said. "We were fighting over my corner." She didn't need to know Ricky's true reasons. "I'm fine. But I have to hurry or I'll be late."

The next morning, I got back home earlier than usual, before Mama and Saara even started breakfast.

"Jussi, what is wrong?" asked Mama, serving me porridge.

"Remember the carrier boy who broke his wrists? He showed up this morning. He got his paper route back. After this long, I was hoping he wouldn't want it anymore." I couldn't shake the feeling that Ricky had something to do with this. I kept rearranging the porridge in my bowl without eating. "Who knows how many years it'll be until I get my own route."

" 'We live as we can, not as we may wish,' " said Mama. It was one of her favourite Finnish proverbs. She patted my shoulder. Then she scraped the last bits from her bowl and headed upstairs. Saara filled the sink to wash the dishes.

I had to get my brain thinking about something else. "Did you see your pal Elias is in the news?"

"What for?" she asked. "Did he crash an ambulance car?"

"No—he got a Distinguished Conduct medal. It says

he was first to volunteer to collect wounded soldiers, while the enemy was still firing."

"I can believe that—he's fearless. Let me see," she said, reaching for the newspaper. She read the whole article. "There were other Canadians honoured, too. You know, the best part of this news is knowing he's still alive."

The second week of school started with a holiday: Labour Day. There wouldn't be the usual Labour Day parade or sports. Nothing was the same during wartime. But it was great weather for a picnic. Last night Mama'd said, "We are overdue for a relaxing outing." My whole family was going to Current River Park for a picnic.

"Jussi, does Fred want to come with us?" asked Mama.

"I don't know where he is, and no one answered my knock next door," I said. "He missed school on Friday. And he hasn't showed up to sell newspapers, either."

"Perhaps he's been sick. You'll likely see him at school tomorrow."

We set out for the streetcar stop. I remembered my last ride to Current River—with Mr. Serious along. Once on board the streetcar, I took a close look at the passengers. Saara believed the spies was long gone, but I sure didn't. Whew—no sign of any suspicious-looking men. Or any disguised as women. Yet the men around us was acting different. They was extra loud, talking and laughing. I caught a word here and there and figured out why they was so jolly.

We climbed down from the streetcar at the park. When we was off on our own a little, Saara asked Papa about the men's conversations. "What is Cow Cash? Is that a new prize for best cow at the Fall Fair?"

My father smiled. I couldn't help it—I belly-laughed. Saara gave me an annoyed look and said, "Papa, tell me what it is."

"It's gold, Saara-*kulta*. A gold strike in the Kowkash River area, northeast of Nipigon." He set down our picnic basket in a shady spot. "They say it's one of the richest ever made in this part of the country." Papa's eyes gleamed. "It's mighty tempting to go stake a claim."

"You're teasing, right?" said Saara.

Papa didn't answer. *He wouldn't really give up his job to gamble on a gold claim, would he?*

Mama found some Finnish friends to visit with. The Port Arthur City Band was playing dancing music. I missed the Fifty-Second Battalion Band. I liked their military march music better.

"Let's go swimming," I said, tugging on Papa's sleeve. We walked a few paces toward the pool.

Then Papa stopped and looked back. "Saara, are you coming?"

"No," she answered. "I'm going to find a tree to sit against and read."

Huzzah! I had Papa all to myself and no danger of my sister repeating what she did on Dominion Day.

Later, we devoured every last crumb of our picnic lunch. We joined the big rush of people heading to the streetcar. Us Mäkis was the last ones to squeeze on board. When we reached our stop, my ears perked up. It was the familiar sound of the Fifty-Second Battalion Band.

The bandsmen was riding in the back of a slow-moving open truck. Banners covered the sides of the truck. Messages on them asked men to join the army. The soldiers marched behind. A black bear cub—their mascot—lumbered along with them. The parade stopped at the corner.

One of the officers climbed onto the truck bed and began his recruiting speech. "Are YOU one of the enervates who loll around in automobiles, the bars, and moving picture shows?" he barked, pointing at a young man on the sidewalk. "Is your backbone so weak you cannot say 'I will fight'?"

I couldn't take my eyes off the bear. A soldier cut up an orange with his pocket knife and fed it to the cub. Then he held a bottle of pop to the bear's mouth so he could drink.

"If you are a MAN," the recruiting officer shouted, "then join the Fifty-Second Battalion and join it now!"

If I was seventeen, or even sixteen, I'd try to convince them I was eighteen and enlist. I'd have to pass the medical examination. But they'd just made that easier, so my weak lungs might not be a problem. At the Co-Op I'd heard talk of conscription. I wasn't sure what that was, so I asked Cam. He said the government might force every man without excuse to become a soldier. Married men didn't even need their wife's permission in writing anymore to enlist.

Back at home, I walked straight to the kitchen for a glass of water. I stopped short in the doorway and called out, "There's broken glass in here!"

"How'd you break a glass so quickly?" asked Saara.

"I didn't. It's window glass."

"What?" said Papa, moving past me. *Crunch*. He stepped on a shard. There was a baseball-sized hole in the window above the sink. Mama gasped.

"What's that under the table?" asked Saara. She pointed to a dark object. It was definitely not a baseball.

Papa crouched. He picked up a jagged grey rock. Tightly wound string held a folded piece of paper against the rock. He tugged at a corner to free the paper and unfolded it. There was handwriting on it. He read the note and swore.

Fear twisted my gut. This wasn't a simple prank.

"What does it say?" asked Mama, a tremor in her voice.

"'Stop union work or be blacklisted. German-loving aliens not welcome.'"

I asked, "What does *blacklisted* mean?"

"That I'd lose my job and no one else would hire me," said Papa, his face turning red. "How dare someone threaten me!"

Ricky'd made sure I knew what that felt like. If Papa was blacklisted, he'd have to leave Port Arthur to get work. Maybe Mama was right that Papa shouldn't go to any more labour meetings. But he sounded more determined than ever to keep going.

CHAPTER 35 | Saara

"Canadians put a rock in the cogs of the German war machine."—The Note Book, *Port Arthur Daily News*, 1915

After school on Tuesday, Mama was cooking rice pudding for supper. We weren't poor—at least not yet. She just wanted to be careful with money. So, for a change, I didn't have to peel potatoes. Instead I settled in with my homework at the kitchen table. I'd written only two paragraphs when John blew in, out of breath.

"Fred's been locked up for five days!" he said, then gulped air.

"Why would his mother lock him up?" I asked.

"No—he's been in jail."

"*Mitä ihmettä?*" asked Mama, her eyebrows furrowed. "Why would they put a boy in jail?"

"For stealing wheat from a railcar to sell. This is the second time Fred and his mother were caught by the railway police. The first time, they just got a harsh talking-to in police court. But if he's caught stealing again, they'll send him to a 're-form-a-tory'! I'm not sure what that is, but it can't be good."

"Are they so hungry they must steal?" said Mama.

"That's why I want to give them some of the money I've earned. Can I, Mama?" pleaded John, reaching for the coffee-tin bank.

"Of course, Jussi."

Pride welled up inside me at my brother's generosity, but I couldn't bring myself to tell him. *God, please help me be less selfish.*

At supper the next day, I poured the dregs from the milk bottle into a dish for Sipu.

John opened the icebox to get another bottle of milk. "What? There's no more!" he said, slamming the door. He grabbed a piece of *näkkileipä* instead. "Why'd you give the last of the milk to Sipu? She doesn't need it—she's getting too fat."

"Sipu's not fat, she's—" But he was gone, crunching the dark rye dried bread on his way outside. I broke off a piece of *näkkileipä* to chew, as well.

Mama's face clouded like an overcast day. "I'm sorry there wasn't more meat in the stew pot. I lost another customer this week."

"Then we should stop pouring money down the drain in rent and buy a house," said Papa. "The prices are dropping so sharply, maybe what we have saved up is enough now."

"I don't know, Tauno," said Mama.

"I know how you can get more sewing business," I said.

"Oh? How is that?" she asked.

"Enter your work in the West Algoma Fall Fair. You're sure to win. Then lots of people will hire you, especially if you put an advertisement in the newspaper like 'First-class sewing done by first-prize winner.'"

Mama didn't say yes, but she didn't say no, either. I could tell she was thinking hard about my suggestion.

"After all of the work I've put into the vegetable garden, I'm going to enter the best carrots and turnips. I can bring your sewing at the same time. The entry fee is only ten cents, and they even want hem stitching. What do you say?"

"I say you'll need to enter the vegetables in John's name, too."

He hadn't done nearly as much work as I had, but it was only fair to include his name.

It was the Thursday before the Fall Fair would open. Mr. Graham announced, "Our esteemed mayor has declared a half holiday for next Thursday, September 16, due—"

A flurry of whispers filled the room.

"—due to it being Port Arthur Day at the Fall Fair. Businesses and schools will be closed for the afternoon."

Raucous cheers exploded.

"However ..." Mr. Graham said, then made us quiet down before continuing. "*However*, the following day, Friday the seventeenth, is *not* a holiday. In fact," he said, looking directly at me, "you are *required* to attend. There will be an in-class essay at the start of the day."

As one, the class groaned.

I received his message loud and clear—if I didn't come to school and complete the work, he might not let me stay in Senior Fourth. *Nothing will keep me away*, I vowed.

After dismissal I rushed home and found Mama scrubbing the kitchen floor. "Stay out until the floor dries," she ordered. Her words halted my steps just in time.

I told her about the half holiday. "Can we go to the Fall Fair?"

"Jussi beat you to asking, and I already told him yes," she replied, smiling over her shoulder.

"Thank you! I know your hem stitching is going to win. If our carrots could grow a bit more, they'll have a good chance."

" 'We live as we can, not as we may wish,' Saara," said Mama. She wrung out her rag. "There's another letter for you, on the parlour table."

Birgitta had written again. I felt a twinge of guilt over not replying to her last letter yet.

Miss Birgitta Schmidt
Vernon, B.C., Canada, Internment Camp,
Sept. 1st, 1915

Dear Saara,
I cannot stop thinking about you and everyone else starting school without me. As soon as you can, please write and tell me everything. Helping the children learn English is hard—they do not try. I will ask the

Y.M.C.A. *people for a book so I can teach myself more English. Or maybe one of the smart adults will give me some lessons. My brain is rotting.*

█████████████████████

██████ *We are fed enough, with plenty of Okanagan fruit—pears, peaches, and apples. I like Jonathans the best, but I miss Northern Spies.* ████████████

████████████████████████

████████████████

    Think back to the middle of July. Do you remember the "project" that got our brothers into trouble when you hurt your ankle? A project is underway here with bigger boys. Someday I will tell you all about it. I want the war to end so we can leave this hot, dusty, dull place. That is all I can think of to write.
    Your loving friend,
    Birgitta

As I read her letter, I became more and more anxious. It sounded like the prisoners were digging a tunnel to escape! Was Birgitta's father involved? What if they were caught? How would they be punished? And why did Birgitta tell me?

My thoughts were flying in all directions at once. This was serious. I should report it—but then what would happen to my friend and her family? I didn't want to get them in trouble. *What should I do?*

"The floor is dry." My body jolted—it was Mama calling. "You can peel the potatoes now."

In the kitchen I found newspaper articles strewn on the table. Usually John clipped them and pasted them in his scrapbook right away. The headline of the nearest article made my breath catch, and I couldn't help reading more.

EXPLOSIVES FOUND ON GRAIN SHIP: Two dumbbell-shaped thin glass bottles containing highly explosive liquid were found on board a grain ship moments before it sailed into Lake Superior. It is alleged that they were positioned such that the motion of the ship would roll the bottles together, causing the glass to break and the liquid to explode, destroying the grain and possibly the entire ship.

The way my heart was pumping and my hands were shaking, I wished I'd resisted reading. It was another plot by saboteurs in Port Arthur, no doubt. John's concerns were real.

At last it was our half-day holiday! When I got to school that morning, everyone was overflowing with energy. Most of the students in my class raised their hand when Mr. Graham asked who was attending the Fall Fair. We had no hope of being let out early; as principal, he had to keep his class there until *exactly* twelve o'clock.

Come noon, we ran out the doors of the school, squealing and laughing. The sky was as clear and bright as our spirits. I ran the whole way home. From the porch, I called out, "Mama, can we leave as soon as Papa gets here?"

"We'll go as soon as we've eaten the lunch I prepared. Why carry it with us when we can have it here?" she reasoned.

"Can we at least leave the dishes for later?" I pleaded. The horse racing would begin at 1:30 p.m., and I didn't want to miss a hoofbeat. "Please?"

"I suppose."

Papa walked in with John right behind. They took their spots at the table and John said, "I can't wait to see the Twirling Talbuts on the trapeze. Won't that be exciting, Papa?"

"I'm sure you'll enjoy the show, Jussi. You can tell me all about it."

"That's because you'll be watching the close finishes on the racetrack with me, won't you?" I said, gloating.

"No, Saara. Today I'm taking full advantage of the quiet house to enjoy a long nap. Then I want to catch up on my work at the library."

"But you'll miss out on all the fun," moaned John.

"There's always next year," said Papa. He often volunteered in the library at the Big Finn Hall. As much as I enjoyed helping him there, I couldn't understand choosing that and sleep over horse racing and all the free attractions.

Mama, John, and I joined the throng on the streetcar heading to the agricultural grounds between the Twin Cities. At the fair, the crowd streamed toward the gate. As we entered the fairgrounds, a clown gripping a cluster of balloons gave a red one to John and an orange one to me. "Before you young 'uns leave today, check your balloons. If you're lucky, you'll find a prize ticket for a one-dollar box of Nyal's Chocolates."

John shook his balloon. "Something's rattling in there." He impatiently popped his balloon and read the message on the paper. "NO PRIZE." I didn't intend to carry a balloon with me all afternoon, so I quickly burst mine, too. No prize for me, either. We added our deflated balloons to the collection in the garbage bin.

"Both of you, meet me right back here at the gate after the horse racing," said Mama. She waved as she headed to the exhibition building to see the fancy work. There'd been plenty of entries already when I'd brought in our vegetables and Mama's sewing earlier in the week.

"I ain't staring at horses running in circles when there's a midway to explore," said John, taking off in the opposite direction.

That suited me fine. I found a seat in the stands as a half-mile heat finished. After two more heats, the announcer introduced the lineup of horses for the Ogilvie Cup. Wilkmer, the winner of the cup last year, was running to defend the title. King Okla had been setting track records in western Canada, so he was one to watch. My cheers were for the girl—Lady May. She'd been beaten on other tracks, but perhaps today was her day to leave everyone else in the dust. The riders manoeuvred their mounts to the starting line.

"No surprise finding you here," said a familiar voice in Finnish.

"Mikko! How did you find me in this crowd?" I said, grinning with delight that he had.

"I have my ways," he said. "Wilkmer's looking in fine shape today."

"You honestly think that plug can win? Lady May's in top form."

"She's sluggish today—see how her head is drooping?"

I whipped around and stared at Lady May. She was tossing her head. Then I heard Mikko chuckle. I whacked him hard on the arm, embarrassed that I'd been duped. "Stop! I get enough of that sort of thing from John."

"A fellow wouldn't treat you that way if he didn't like you."

I could have fried bacon on my cheeks.

"They're off!" boomed the heavyset man to my left.

I was riveted on the horses thundering around the track. "Come on, Lady May!" I shouted.

"Go, Wilkmer!" roared Mikko on my right *and* the man on my left. I was surrounded—but not silenced. I cheered all the louder.

Sadly, Wilkmer beat Lady May by a nose. Actually, I was certain it was only by a nostril.

In the din, Mikko leaned over to speak in my ear. "She made Wilkmer stretch. It was her best race all year. Likely pushed Wilkmer to set a new track record."

That eased my disappointment a little.

"Can I buy you an ice cream?" he asked.

I smiled. "Of course."

We fought our way through the hordes of fairgoers to the ice cream stand, waited forever in the lineup, and finally slurped our cold treats.

Suddenly I remembered Mama's orders and grabbed Mikko's sleeve, pointing to the main gate. "Run!"

It was a tricky business dodging people and keeping our ice cream cones intact. Mama and John were waiting at the gate. She stood with her arms crossed, and John wore a scowl. At the sight of us, John rolled his eyes.

"I see why you forgot to meet us," said Mama, shaking her head. "Hello, Mikko. How are you and your family?"

"Everyone is swell, Mrs. Mäki. I'm sorry for distracting Saara."

John said to Mikko, "You want to watch the vaudeville acts with us? Or do you and my sister want to be alone?"

I ignored his tease.

"I can't miss the Talbuts," said Mikko. "I've heard their act is top-notch."

"Let's go," called John, already running toward the grandstand.

We wove through the crowd. On stage, the Blackstone Quartette were singing their soulful tunes. I stared in fascination at their dark skin. Next up was the act John most itched to see: the Twirling Talbuts on the trapeze and rings. Their amazing feats mesmerized us. Then came a pedestal act, acrobatic tricks with a dog, and a lady foot juggler. My palms stung from clapping so hard.

When the Blackstone Quartette returned to the stage, we left to see more of the fair.

"Mikko, the Fifty-Second is doing their musket drill now," said John.

"Enjoy that, John. I'm off to inspect the horses. Saara, do you want to join me?"

"For sure. I'll check on our vegetable entries later." I was itching to leave my teasing brother behind.

"I would be better off if I hadn't gone to see the sewing," said Mama.

"Why is that?" I asked.

"The other entries are far fancier than mine."

"Well, 'we live as we can, not as we may wish,' Mama."

The way she wrinkled her nose told me she'd rather live as she wished—winning first prize. Back to wearing her no-nonsense face, Mama said, "After the band concert, meet me at the gate again."

In the horse barn, Mikko and I wandered from stall to stall admiring powerful workhorses and sleek race-horses. One of the fine-boned racehorses set his teeth on the stall door and sucked in great gulps of air.

"He's sure a nervous one," said Mikko. "Canadian horses are superior—even tempers, thick bodies—"

"Strong bones, amazing endurance. I know, I know," I said, chuckling. "You've told me a thousand times. Come on—I want to see the winner of the pony race."

Partway along the row of ponies, he said, "Aleksandra came to the fair yesterday, but I doubt she set foot in here. She seems a whole lot happier than when I last saw her. Thank you for spending time with her."

"Are you sure it's the time with me that's changed her mood, or time with Jim?"

"Who's Jim?"

"A fellow who's sweet on her and buys her nougatines."

"She never breathed a word. Tell me everything you know."

That took me all of one minute. "Anything more, you'll have to ask your sister."

Outside, the Fifty-Second Battalion Band struck up the opening song of their concert. "That's my signal," said Mikko. "I have to get back to Port Arthur."

"Oh, too bad. I was hoping you'd come see our first-place carrots and turnips."

"Congratulations," he said, holding out his hand to shake mine. Then he pulled it back. "Wait a minute. Judging's not until tonight. You tricked me." As quick as a wink he tied my braids in a knot. "I'd say we're even now."

I grinned. "Thanks for finding me today. It was great to see you again."

"It was a whole lot more fun than taking in the fair by myself." Mikko swooped in and kissed my cheek. "Goodbye," he said, leaving for the gate.

I stood rooted in happy confusion, my hand up to my face. Did kissing my cheek mean he was now my beau? It would be too awkward to ask his sister, and Helena was not approachable. I'd never write it in a letter to Birgitta for the censor to read. The question would need to wait until I next wrote to Auntie.

In a daze, I entered the exhibition building. A wave of floral perfume met me. Shelf after shelf held flowers of every shape and colour. Tables were crammed with food entries: pickles, jellies, and preserves. Sheaves of wheat, barley, rye, and oats stood ready for examination. In one display were giant black berries that looked like raspberries. Not surprisingly, these new-to-me fruits were called blackberries.

Finally I reached the vegetables. Green Hubbard squash contrasted with clean white potatoes. Beans on the stalk were next to several varieties of corn, lettuce, and turnips. *Yes,* there was our turnip entry, and my name was even spelled right for a change. Around the corner stood a table loaded with carrots. Everyone in the Twin Cities must have entered a sample. First prize would definitely not go to our small specimens. But there was still hope for our turnips.

I went outside to check whether the band concert was over and heard the strains of "O Canada," likely their final number. That was good timing. I sprinted to the gate to make sure I got there ahead of my brother. Mama appeared within seconds after the final bars of "O Canada" died away.

"Hello, Saara. Did you agree with the judges' decisions about the horses?"

"Yes—now if only the sewing and vegetable judges are equally fair."

"'It is good to live in hope,'" said Mama, quoting another Finnish proverb.

CHAPTER 36 | John

"After comparing the produce of our vegetable gardens
with the pictures on the cover of the seed catalogue
we are bound to admit that pictures speak louder than
vegetables."—The Note Book, *Port Arthur Daily News*,
1915

I ran up to Mama and Saara, saying, "I'm starving. Can I
have a hot dog? They're only five cents."

Last year at the fair, the sellers called them frankfurters
and charged ten cents. With all the bad feelings against
Germany (and suspicion of enemy aliens), they dropped
the German name. It must not have been enough to make
them sell 'cause they dropped the price, too.

Mama splurged on hot dogs *and* ginger ale for us.
We found a spot out of the way to eat and drink. Judging
was still going on, so when we was done, we wandered
around.

"We could go see the champion dogs," suggested
Saara.

"I'm not getting any closer to a 'dog' than my supper,"
I said.

People was flocking into the exhibition building. We

guessed the judging was over now. It was so crowded on the first floor, we went straight upstairs to the ladies' fancy work. Mama's hem stitching won first prize! A huge smile spread across her face.

"I knew you would win," said Saara. "That should bring you more customers. Now you can advertise 'Sewing by West Algoma Fall Fair first-prize winner.'"

We returned to the first floor. "Drat," said Saara. "Our carrots didn't even win an honourable mention. But look at our turnips, John!"

"Second place!" I cheered.

Saara grinned. "That's exceptional for beginner farmers, I'd say."

Mama hugged my sister and me, saying, "Well done, you two!" Then she let out a big yawn. "It's time we went home."

The fair wasn't closing for another hour, but she looked really tired. I decided not to argue. The sun was setting as we trudged to the streetcar and slumped in our seats. Soon after the streetcar began to move, Mama leaned against the window and nodded off.

A while later, I saw a bright flash. "What was that?" I exclaimed, startling Mama awake.

"What happened?" she asked.

"Lightning, I think," said Saara. "It came out of nowhere. But I don't hear any thunder, and there's no rain." She frowned.

"Very strange," said Mama.

I stared out the window, expecting more lightning, but there was none.

We was almost at our stop when something bright and orangey-yellow caught my eye. It was a huge flame! Then I heard the clanging of the fire engine bell.

"Look over there!" I cried, pointing to the fire lighting up the dark sky. "I think it's the grain elevator." I stood on the seat to get a better view. "I bet it was sabotaged!"

"Don't be ridiculous," scoffed Saara. "The lightning probably started the blaze." She got to her feet next to me to see the burning grain elevator.

The streetcar braked. I wiggled around Saara, saying, "I'm going to get a closer look." I was stepping down to the ground when Mama said, "Stop him, Saara!"

My sister grabbed the back of my coat.

"No, Jussi," Mama ordered. "It's too dangerous."

I stopped. There was no point trying to change her mind when she used *that* tone of voice. I shrugged off Saara's hand.

We stood there, dumbstruck, staring at the sky getting brighter and brighter.

Too soon, Mama said, "Time to go."

We headed toward home.

I kept trying to catch another glimpse as we walked. "I wonder what really started the fire?"

"The flames grew so tall, so fast," said Saara.

"I hope they can put it out quickly," said Mama, "before all the grain is lost."

After two blocks, the breeze started picking up. *Splat.* A cold raindrop hit the back of my neck. We walked faster as the raindrops increased.

As we reached our back lane, a steady rain was falling.

We was almost at our house. It looked like the porch light was on. Papa must be home. There was so much to tell him—the fire at the elevator, and all about the Fall Fair.

Then I heard a shout. Was it from inside our house? Again someone shouted, but I couldn't make out the words.

"*Mitä ihmettä?*" asked Mama.

Something wasn't right. We rounded the corner of our house. There was a big black square shape out front.

"What's that?" asked Saara.

The porch light lit the side of the motor-powered wagon. I saw big white letters. "POLICE PATROL."

"Wh-why are the police here?" asked Saara.

I felt queasy.

The door of our house opened. A policeman stepped out, shining a flashlight. I was blinded for a moment.

Then another officer came out carrying a flashlight. He was dragging Papa with him!

Mama gasped.

Now both policemen was manhandling Papa. They steered him toward the back of the patrol wagon.

Papa wrenched his arms from their grasp. The shorter officer dropped his flashlight. He bent to retrieve it.

Papa stood his ground, demanding, "What is this all about?"

"Tauno Mäki, you are under arrest," stated the other officer.

Both men grabbed Papa and dragged him closer to the patrol wagon. One policeman opened the rear door.

"NO!" cried Mama, darting forward. "Let him go!" In Finnish she said, "Tauno, what happened?"

"This is a mistake," said Papa in English.

Saying nothing, the police officers forced Papa into the back of the patrol wagon.

Papa called out to us in Finnish, "I've done nothing wrong."

I ran to one of the policemen. "He's not an enemy alien. He's Finnish."

"We know, lad. We've been watching him."

"But he's my father," I said.

Saara asked, "Why are you taking him?"

From inside the black truck, Papa called, "Is this about union organizing?"

The taller policeman banged the door shut and locked it. "Constable Brown," he said gruffly, "carry out the orders while I stand guard." Papa kept demanding answers, but his words was muffled.

Constable Brown turned to Mama and said, "Ma'am, I must search the premises." He walked back into our house.

Mama looked stunned. She said nothing. Me and Saara pulled her out of the rain and wind into the porch. She refused to go farther inside the house. Staring through the porch window at the patrol wagon, she sobbed and prayed out loud nonstop.

Me and Saara ran into the house. We got to the kitchen in time to see the policeman open the door to the basement and clomp down the wooden steps.

I whispered to Saara, "What's he searching for?"

"I don't know."

Before long the constable returned. He snooped through the kitchen cupboards and drawers. He searched the parlour, then headed toward the stairs.

We started to follow him. He turned around and said, "Stay down here while I comb the second storey."

We sank onto the bottom step. The officer's heavy footsteps circled our parents' bedroom, then Saara's, and then mine.

"I don't understand why they're arresting Papa," I said.

"It makes no sense," said Saara. "It's just like it was when they arrested Fred's dad and Mr. Schmidt."

Looking her in the eyes, I was pretty sure she was as scared as me and was thinking the same thing as me: *What if they send Papa away, too?*

At the sound of the constable's boots on the stairs, we leaped to our feet. He passed between us lugging a tower of papers and envelopes and books. I tried to see what he took. There was my scrapbook! And my books about science, weapons, and technology. What did he want them for?

"That's just my scrapbook," I called after him, "and my library books."

At the front door, Constable Brown said, "It's all evidence and will be held as long as necessary." He charged through the porch and straight to the patrol wagon to stow what he'd taken.

We collected Mama and followed him outside. Raindrops blew in our faces. I shielded my eyes with one hand.

The other policeman stood on the rear platform of the patrol wagon and asked, "Anything more?"

"I heard them talking about Carl Schmidt, and I found a bullet casing from a revolver." He jumped behind the steering wheel and started the engine. The patrol wagon pulled away, heading to the city jail.

Our father was gone.

"We can't grow men fast enough."—*Port Arthur Daily News*, 1915

John glared at me. "That was dumb to say the name *Schmidt*." He gave me a hard shove. "You just made everything a whole lot worse."

"What about you, saving that bullet casing?" I kicked his shin.

"Ow!" he yelped.

"Come on—we have to get Mama inside."

Mama stared after the patrol wagon as it turned from our side lane onto Foley Street. "It's a mistake," she mumbled. "It's all a mistake."

I reached my arm around Mama, saying, "Let's get out of the rain." I guided her into the porch.

Mama moaned. "What if he loses his job? Then what are we going to do?"

John said, "Let's go dry out in the kitchen, Mama."

"And warm up," I added. "I'll make you some tea."

Inside the kitchen, Mama collapsed onto a chair.

I built up the fire in the wood stove and set the kettle to boil. "Can you find her shawl, John?"

He fetched Mama's shawl from the parlour. I wrapped it around her shoulders.

"I want to see what all is missing," said John. He dashed upstairs.

I got out the Red Rose tea and rinsed the teapot.

When John returned, he said, "They even took my budget and my pile of newspaper clippings! Why do they care about them?"

"Those don't matter one bit," I said. "We have to focus on getting Papa out of jail."

"Then let's go there right now and find out why they arrested him," said John.

"Now?" exclaimed Mama. "It's too late to get there and back by streetcar, and I don't think my legs could carry me that far. Saara and I will take the first streetcar in the morning."

"What about me?" John asked. "I'm almost ten, and I'm the man of the house now."

"*Kiitos*, Jussi, but you have newspapers to sell in the morning. And I need you to let Papa's employer know he can't work for a day or two. Do not say he was arrested— say there's been an emergency. Now off you go to bed."

He didn't argue.

When the water boiled, I brewed the tea. I handed a steaming cup to Mama.

"*Kiitos*," she said. "Now you go to sleep, too, Saara. I'll be up for a while."

I tossed and turned on my mattress. This was no ordinary night—my father was in jail.

CHAPTER 38 | John

"Pretty soon we'll be hearing rumors about the
Northern Spy, when it will be in order to put in as many
barrels of espionage as we can afford."
—The Note Book, *Port Arthur Daily News,* 1915

My Big Ben rang and I jumped out of bed. My stomach
churned. It wasn't 'cause I was hungry. It was 'cause I was
so worried. What was happening to Papa?

I got dressed quickly and headed outside, down the
back lane. It was still damp from last night's rain.

Whenever I hawked newspapers, I had to talk to
strangers all the time. So why was I feeling so awful
nervous about talking to Papa's boss? I guessed part of
it was needing to be careful *not* to say things. All the way
there I practised what *to* say.

When I arrived, Papa's boss was asking the other men
if anyone knew where Tauno was. "He's never missed
work before." No one gave an answer.

"I'm his son and he ain't coming today," I said. "We've
had an emergency."

"Anything we can help with?" asked one of the
workers.

His kindness choked me up a little. "No ... uh ... we can handle it," I said, trying to sound brave. "But thank you, sir."

I ran off before they could ask me any more questions that would be tough to answer. Partway to the *Daily News* building, I up and changed my mind. At top speed, I headed back home. Could I catch Mama and Saara before they left?

I saw them turn into the back lane as I passed the Pekkonens' boarding house. They was coming my way.

Mama spotted me and called out, "Jussi, what are you doing back here already?"

I waited until we was closer to each other so I wouldn't have to yell. "I talked to Papa's boss. But I decided I can miss one Friday of selling papers. Please, I want to come with you."

"No, Jussi," said Mama. "Saara and I will deal with—"

"Today is Friday!" Saara interrupted. "Mama, I can't ..."

"You can't what, Saara?" asked Mama.

"I can't miss school today," said my sister. This sounded serious. "There's an essay I have to write."

"Is a few hours of school more important than doing everything we can to free Papa? I need you to translate for me."

Saara opened her mouth to speak, but nothing came out. I could tell she was thinking mighty hard, like she couldn't decide what to do. Then she said, "You're right, Mama. I have to go with you."

"No, you don't," I said, bent on convincing both of them. "Go to school, Saara—I can translate for Mama."

"But—"

I switched to English. "Look, I don't want to get in your way anymore. Go do what you need to do at school. I can handle this."

She smiled. "Thanks, Johnny."

Me and Mama sped down the hill and boarded the streetcar. I wanted to jump out and push so it would roll faster. What had the night in jail been like for Papa? Had they fed him anything? What if they really did send him to Kapuskasing? How would we get by if Papa wasn't working?

We got off at the stop closest to the city jail and walked to the large stone building. We was so early, the door was still locked. Mama lowered herself onto a step. I paced.

Finally we heard the click of the lock. We could go in.

"Hello, sir," I said to the man who unlocked the door. "We want to see Mr. Tauno Mäki."

"Is he the bloke who torched the grain last night?" he replied.

Torched the grain? The police think Papa started that fire at the grain elevator? I was shocked that they'd accuse Papa of being a sabotager. I hurried to translate his words into Finnish for Mama. Her cheeks turned white.

I said to the man, "He was arrested last night, but he would never set fire to grain."

"Sorry, lad. He's off limits. No visitors allowed."

"But we must see him. We have to find out where he was before he was arrested."

"Told you—he tried to burn down the elevator below Bay Street."

"You don't understand. He's my father and he's innocent."

"They'll determine all that in court, lad." He stared at me, squinting. "Say, are you the fellow who dumped yer spuds in the road this summer? You and yer sister were dragging a handcart near the Coca-Cola bottling works?"

"Yes, sir, that was me. Are you—?"

"Joseph's the name." To Mama he said, "Are you his mother?"

"Yes."

"Look, ma'am, I shouldn't be telling you this, but I don't hold much hope for your husband. 'Tis a shame—he seems like a decent man."

Flustered, Mama said, "Tell Jussi" as she pulled me in front of her. "He has good English."

"Well, lad, 'tis like this," he said, lowering his voice. "I heard there is correspondence between your address and interned enemy aliens."

"That was my sister," I said. "She's been writing to her friend in the Vernon camp."

"'Tis an inordinate amount of correspondence for schoolgirls. 'Tis a cover-up for conspiratorial communication, they think."

"No, sir, it's not," I said in horror. "If they'd read them they'd see."

"Oh, they've been read, all right. Railway details, reference to 'Northern Spies'—most likely the kind who carry dynamite—writing in code."

What was my sister up to?

Joseph kept talking. "'Tis jail for your father till he

242

goes before the magistrate," he said, shaking his head and turning away. "'Tis a shame."

I felt like I was going to puke all over the floor. Somehow I remembered to be polite. "Thank you."

"Yer mighty welcome. So long, now."

I translated everything for Mama. Stunned, we set off for home.

A familiar motorcar was driving toward us. It was Cam's. "Mama, you go on ahead and I'll catch up. I want to ask Cam, I mean Mr. Cameron, something."

Mama kept plodding.

With both arms I signalled to Cam to stop. I ran up to the driver's side. "Cam, I need your help bad. My father was arrested last night and—"

"Hold on, Scoop. Are you talking about the sabotage? That was your father?"

"He didn't do it, Cam. He—"

But Cam held up his hand to stop me. "I can't get involved. If I did, the police wouldn't give me tips."

"Is that the truth or are you umbrellishing the facts again?" I snapped.

Cam chuckled.

I clenched my fists. "Don't laugh—this ain't funny!"

"You're right," he said, wiping the smile off his face.

"So you're saying getting the story is more important than helping me?"

"Sorry, Scoop. I want to help you, but I can't risk it, pal."

"You ain't my pal anymore." I charged after Mama. It was a quiet streetcar ride and quieter walk.

Saara must've heard us coming 'cause she met us at the

door with the morning newspaper. "It says a Port Arthur man was arrested for sabotaging the grain elevator—do they mean ..." She gulped. "Do they mean Papa?"

I had no words so I just nodded, my eyes getting watery. It was too horrible that the paper was talking about our father like he was a criminal.

Mama said, "I thought you would still be at school. Did you finish your essay?"

"I got it done, and then I tried to do mathematics. But my brain wouldn't function, thinking about Papa. So I pretended I was sick and left. I'm sorry I fibbed, Mama."

Mama hugged her and said, "I'm glad you're here. You, too, Jussi." She drew me into the hug, too. "Thank you for coming to the jail with me."

"You're welcome," I said. Mama finally let go.

"How is he, Mama?" asked Saara.

"I don't know. They wouldn't let us see him."

Between me and Mama we filled my sister in on what had happened.

"Can I have that?" I asked, reaching for the newspaper. The article stated: *"Following an explosion, militia guarding the grain elevator smelled smoke. Upon investigation, the soldier spotted the saboteur in a black coat escaping on foot. The soldier fired, and the arsonist returned shots with a revolver. By the time the guard had telephoned the fire department and police, the saboteur was out of sight. Firemen quickly extinguished the flames, preventing the elevator from burning to the ground. Police officers scoured the neighbourhood. Witnesses along Bay Street confirmed the direction in which the saboteur fled, allowing the police to track his footprints. They succeeded in recovering his weapon. The suspect is under arrest and in custody in the city jail."*

How much had Cam invented for his report? All we knew for sure was there was an explosion and a fire, and there was an innocent man in jail. "Will you believe me now, Saara?" I pleaded. "There is *still* a sabotager around here."

"Yes, John. I definitely believe you."

CHAPTER 39 | Saara

"What would be required to shock the world today?"
—The Note Book, *Port Arthur Daily News*, 1915

John kept staring at the newspaper report about the saboteur. In my mind I was replaying *The Girl Detective*, the one where Scotty Weed was trying to establish his alibi. That's what Papa needed me to do. But this was no moving picture—it was real and terrifying to have my own father arrested for a crime. I started thinking out loud. "Now I have to figure out where Papa was last night when the grain elevator was set on fire, so I can prove his alibi."

"What do you mean, 'I'?" asked John. "We can work together to get the alley-by or whatever you called it."

"Okay, then, help me think this through. What did Papa say he was going to do instead of coming to the Fall Fair with us?"

"He was gonna have a nap, then go do some work at the library at the Big Finn Hall."

"That's where we should start," I said. "Mama, we're going to find out how long Papa was working in the library last night."

"All right," said Mama, sounding distracted. She continued scrubbing a pot she'd already cleaned.

Mr. Campbell stopped raking and stared as we ran past. He didn't say hello. Was he one of the witnesses who'd pointed the police toward our house?

Outside the Finnish Labour Temple—the Big Finn Hall—a number of Finnish men were gathered. Their conversation stopped abruptly at the sight of us, so I had a good idea what they were discussing. Word must have gotten around about the patrol wagon being at our house.

"Hello—were any of you here last night between eight and nine o'clock?" I asked.

"I was home all night," "Not me," and "I was at the fair" were the answers they gave. Even if any of the men *had* been here, would the police take the word of one Finlander for another? I wasn't sure it would be enough proof.

"Let's go inside, John." We climbed the stairs to the library of Finnish books. If only we'd find Papa working there now, instead of being locked away in the jail. I felt a wave of panic. *God, we need your help.*

The library room was quiet. I checked Papa's record book. "The last few titles are all dated September 16, in Papa's handwriting. So he *was* here yesterday."

"Did he sign his name?" asked John.

"No."

"Then the police won't believe he was here."

"You're right." Gooseflesh covered my arms as I thought again about how serious this was for Papa. "We need solid proof of where he was when the grain elevator was sabotaged." I gulped. "We have to fix this terrible mistake."

I shuffled through the papers on the desk, checking for something—anything—else. My pulse raced as I uncovered a page of yesterday's newspaper. "I found something."

"What is it?"

I pointed to the notice in the centre that was circled. It was for the sale by public auction of a two-storey frame house on the same street as our church. "Do you think Papa went there to bid yesterday? He's been talking about house prices getting closer to what we can afford."

"Look at the time—half past seven last night, which means—"

"If Papa was there, he couldn't have been at the grain elevator! We need to talk to the man in charge. He would have a record of who registered to bid and the list of auction bids." I studied the notice, looking for his name.

Mr. Douglas McLeod.

"NO!" I cried.

"What's wrong?"

"It's Mr. McLeod. Of all people!"

"You mean the McLeods you worked for?"

"Yes, and he's the one man I dare not show my face to ever again."

"Why? What did you do?"

Drat and double drat. Mama never told him why I'd lost my job, and now I had to admit to him how I had masqueraded as the English girl Sarah McKee. I choked down my pride and confessed.

"You really are a good actor, aren't you?"

That wasn't what I'd expected him to say. "Sure."

Now we needed to focus on our predicament. I began thinking out loud again. "How can I get that bid information without speaking to Mr. McLeod? If he finds out why I need his witness he won't want to help. He might think, *Like daughter, like father*, that maybe Papa has an alternate identity, like I had. I don't know what to do."

"*I'll* go talk to him," said my brother with unusual determination. He seemed to have suddenly grown more mature.

But could John be trusted to get the information we needed to prove Papa's alibi? Would Mr. McLeod connect John to me? Then hope would be lost.

"Well, Saara?"

"I'm thinking." Could John handle this crucial assignment? As much as I doubted his ability to carry it through, I had no choice. I could not go. *He must go.*

"Okay, John, but you need to pay attention," I said with urgency. "If we can prove he was there at the time the grain elevator was sabotaged, perhaps the police will let him out of jail."

"So you want me to ask Mr. McLeod to check his records to see if Papa made a bid, right?"

"Yes, John. Don't forget to get it in writing."

"Yup."

"Are you sure you can do this?"

"Of course I can—you can trust me, Saara."

The trouble was, I didn't trust him. There were far too many reasons for me not to. But we had to try.

"Oh, no," said John.

"What's wrong?"

"What do I say if he asks why I need to know?"

I dreamed up several explanations, but none were based on the facts. They would only get us into more trouble. "You'll have to tell the truth."

"Then for sure he won't help us Finlanders. This is dumb."

"It will work," I said with confidence I didn't feel. It had to work. "We'll go to his office now."

"Wait—I haven't eaten anything since breakfast—"

"You can eat later. It's Friday afternoon. If Mr. McLeod leaves his office early, we'll have to wait until Monday. By then the newspapers will publish Papa's name. No, we have to do this *right away*."

CHAPTER 40 | John

"Don't worry! German spies cannot last forever!"
—The Note Book, *Port Arthur Daily News*, 1915

"Then let's go find Mr. McLeod, Saara," I said firmly, pulling my sister at a trot down the hill.

We kept up a steady pace all the way to Cumberland Street.

"Mr. McLeod's office should be in this block," said Saara. She began checking for the address. She stopped in front of a three-storey brick building. "Okay, John. This is it."

"I know this place," I said. "Sell newspapers in here all the time."

"Good. So you know where to find the board that'll have his office number."

"Aren't you coming in?" I wished my voice didn't wobble the way it did.

"No, you're on your own. I don't want to risk being seen with you and ruining our chances. Now go," she said, nudging me toward the door. "You can do this."

I flung open the front door of the building. Sucking in a deep breath, I plunged inside. The sign said Mr. McLeod's office was three floors up. I hustled up the steps. I practised over and over what to say as I climbed the last steps to the third floor.

Then I tried to get past the secretary. She said, "Stop right there. Mr. McLeod is busy completing paperwork from last night's auction."

"That's what I need to see him about."

"I'm sorry. He is not to be disturbed."

"It's important."

"You will need to come back on Monday."

Only a few minutes after leaving Saara, I was back on the sidewalk. I glanced right and left several times, searching for her. She stepped out of a shady nook and waved me over.

"What happened?" she said. "You couldn't possibly have seen him and gotten the information this fast. Oh, I wish I could just do this myself—"

"Stop and let me talk!" I roared. "The secretary wouldn't let me see him. So what do I do now?"

"Did you tell her it was important?"

"Oh, yes, but she refused to budge."

"Arrrg! What do we do now?"

"Look, there's Fred," I said, pointing to the other side of the street. I dodged traffic, crossing to where Fred was hawking an Extra. I was back quick as a flash. "Maybe this will get me past the secretary," I said, waving a newspaper in Saara's face. "Mr. McLeod usually buys one." I re-entered the building.

The newspaper worked like a charm. The secretary handed me payment and said, "How did you know that is the only interruption he said he would allow?" She waved me through.

Mr. McLeod barely looked up. "Uh … yes … thank you. Place it on the chair."

"I have to ask you something, sir. About the auction."

"What is it?"

"I need proof in writing that my father, Tauno Mäki, was at the auction last night." I held my breath, hoping Mr. McLeod would say the words I wanted to hear.

"He was indeed there. Mr. Mäki didn't win the auction, but he did make a bid close to the end. He became upset when he couldn't afford to bid any higher and lost the house to someone else." Mr. McLeod shared whatever other details he could remember. Then he said, "Tell me, why do you need proof?"

I explained. He didn't look pleased. After thinking it over, he said, "All right. I'll do it. But if you weren't such a dependable newsboy, I wouldn't be doing this for you. I will write a statement and deliver it to the police tomorrow."

"Thank you very much, sir!" I raced down the flights of stairs to my sister, wearing a huge grin.

"Did you get the proof?" she asked.

"No, but—"

"What do you mean, no? Why are you smiling, then? What are we—?"

"Will you let me finish? Mr. McLeod said Papa was for sure at the auction, and tomorrow he'll write it down and bring it to the police."

"Hurrah!" she exclaimed, giving me a quick hug. "Let's

hightail it before he comes out, sees me talking to you, and decides he won't help Papa after all."

Once me and Saara was a couple blocks away, my heartbeat finally was normal.

Saara mussed my hair and giggled. "Thank you, Johnny. I was praying for you, and you got the job done."

"You didn't really pray for me, did you?"

"Of course I did. I believe God helps us if we ask."

"Keep asking," I said, turning onto Secord Street, "'cause we know Papa didn't start the fire, so the sabotag—saboteur is still out there somewhere."

She muttered, "You're right. Now what would the Girl Detective do to find him?"

Without talking, we kept heading toward home.

We met Mama coming out of the porch. Her eyes all around was red. She said, "I'm going to ask Mr. Pekkonen for advice. I'll be back soon."

In our kitchen, we each drank half a gallon of water and ate our fill of bread and cheese.

I started rereading the report on the sabotage. "No!"

"What's wrong now?"

I pointed to the second paragraph. "The sabotage was discovered at quarter past eight. Mr. McLeod said Papa stormed out when the final bid was accepted—a little before eight o'clock. His statement isn't going to prove Papa wasn't at the grain elevator!"

Saara slumped in her chair. "Now what?"

"The paper says witnesses saw the saboteur run up our back lane. We should have a close look around out there."

My sister perked up. "Great idea."

We darted outside. Saara checked the back lane. I studied the ground by the porch. There was a skid mark next to the house. I pictured the saboteur trying to escape. It was raining and dark. He was running fast. If he'd turned this corner at top speed, then ... *oh!*

"Saara, come here!" She ran over. I pointed at the skid mark. "I think the saboteur slipped and fell here, but kept going. Papa must have gotten home right before the other man ran up here."

"There's part of a boot print!" said Saara. "Let's search the area."

We scoured our side lane, edge to edge, from the back lane to Foley Street. There was no other clues.

"With all the rain overnight there won't be any footprints in the open," said Saara, sounding disappointed.

At the front of our house, I noticed trampled grass next to the foundation. It was in a spot at the corner that was sheltered by the roof. "Someone was here while it was raining."

"But where did he go next?" wondered Saara. "Let's look over our whole backyard."

"Okay." My heart was pounding at the thought that the saboteur had been right next to our house.

Saara checked inside the shelter where Uncle Arvo tied up his workhorses when he came to visit us. I snooped all around the outside. We inspected the grass, then the thorny hedge. It grew between our backyard and the Entwhistles' place. I found a broken branch midway along. Carefully we spread the prickly branches apart and could see more broken pieces farther in. Someone who didn't know about the thorns had cut through here.

A bit of black cloth caught my eye. I snaked my arm into the hedge and pulled it free. "It looks an awful lot like a pocket from a coat," I said, handing it to Saara. My backbone tingled. We had evidence!

I crashed through the hedge. Thorns raked my arms, but I didn't care. Reaching our vegetable garden, I called, "He landed on the potato mounds and flattened part!"

"Wait there—I'm coming around." Saara sprinted off.

I studied the garden. Saara was coming past the shed. I asked her, "Didn't you tell me not to pull all the carrots?"

"Yes—I wanted to choose the best for the Fall Fair."

"Well, they're all gone!"

The shed door flew open. A large hand clamped over Saara's mouth. A man hauled her backward into the shed.

"*Junge,*" he hissed, "boy, get over here or I vill hurt her."

My eyes bulged. Saara turned pale. My legs felt frozen.

"*Komm schnell!*" the man barked.

I startled and moved closer to the shed door.

"Get in," ordered the man. "Close ze door."

He spoke with an accent like Peter's father—a German accent! Was he Mr. Serious from the streetcar? No, Mr. Serious was bulkier, with hair much lighter brown.

The man limped and spewed what sounded like a swear word. He shoved Saara to the ground. "Stay zere."

He pointed at me. "You vill bring me Aspirin and food," he commanded. "You vill tell no von—NO VON—I am here. Ze girl vill stay. Now go!" He had lowered his rough voice, but its power made me run.

CHAPTER 41 | Saara

"One thing to be said for Germany is that she is doing her best to make war unpopular."—The Note Book, *Port Arthur Daily News*, 1915

Be quick, John!

The saboteur shifted to lean against the shed wall and winced. Pain carved deep lines in his brow. He bent to rub his left ankle. When he had fallen by our house, he must have injured his foot. That was why he hadn't run any farther. He smelled of sweat and dirt and carrots.

Fear rose inside me. I had to fight it. I racked my brain trying to think what the Girl Detective would do. Somehow we had to get the police. Once the police had him, they'd know Papa was innocent.

Should I use the few German words I know from Birgitta and pretend to be German? Will he release me? I didn't know enough to be convincing.

Then I remembered what John had retrieved from the hedge. I stared at his coat. Its right pocket was missing.

"Put eyes down," he commanded.

I dropped my gaze. In my head I again heard his harsh threat, "I vill hurt her."

The man slammed his fist into his palm and muttered, "Vhere is zat boy?"

Fear was winning. *Fight back.*

Finally John returned. He thrust bread, cheese, and a bottle of Aspirin at the saboteur.

The man was ravenous, biting off a chunk of cheese. Then he fumbled with the lid of the Aspirin bottle and swore.

John inched toward the long-handled shovel propped against the wall.

The man removed the lid and shook some Aspirin tablets into his hand. He popped them in his mouth, scooped water out of the watering can, and gulped. He coughed—the Aspirin must have stuck in his throat—so he grabbed the watering can and tipped it up to take a drink.

John snatched the shovel and swung the blade full force on the man's head. He dropped the watering can and slumped to the ground. I leaped to my feet.

"Roll him onto his stomach," ordered John.

I didn't argue. The man was heavy. It took all of my strength to turn him over.

John rummaged in the corner and found a length of rope. He flipped open his pocket knife and cut the rope in two, handing one piece to me. "Tie his wrists together tight and be quick!" As I did, John tied the man's ankles. When he yanked hard on the knot, the man groaned.

"Faster, Saara!"

"Done," I said.

"You stand guard—I'll go for the police."

"No, I'll go."

"Look at me—I'm too puny to stop him. Only you can handle staying here."

I did not like the idea of having to stay here one more second with the saboteur. But John's argument made sense, as I was a lot bigger than my brother. "Okay—but run and get your camera first. In case he escapes, we'll have proof."

John ducked out, leaving the shed door wide open. Sunlight streamed in. Minutes passed. Our prisoner's arm twitched. *Hurry, John!*

I could hear footsteps. John rushed in. He quickly snapped two pictures and dashed off.

The man shifted his legs and groaned loudly.

What if he came to? What if the ropes weren't tight enough? What if he got loose?

I stepped to the doorway. Grabbing the shovel, I tensed, ready to knock him out in case he tried to get away.

How long would it take the police to come? *God, please bring them quickly.*

I battled against panic. I tried saying multiplication tables in my head, but that only made things worse. Instead, I recited over and over poems I'd memorized for school.

The man grunted and twisted his hands.

No! The rope I'd tied as tightly as possible was loosening.

In an instant, his hands were free.

I swung the shovel hard, but he shifted away. The

blade thumped the dirt floor. He grabbed the handle, yanking it from my grasp.

I bolted like a spooked horse. My feet pounded the back lane as I ran down the hill.

John was leaping down the back steps of the Pekkonens' boarding house. Mama and Helena's father scurried after him.

"Saara, the Pekkonens have a telephone now," yelled John, "and they called the police and they're on their way. Hey, why'd you leave him? You're supposed to be guarding him!"

"He got his hands loose!"

"We can't let him get away," he urged, dragging me back uphill. Mama and Mr. Pekkonen followed on our heels.

As we reached the Entwhistles' backyard, three police officers rounded the corner of our house into the back lane. John waved to them, saying, "Constable Bryant, over here. The German man is in the shed." The door of the shed still stood ajar.

"What game are you playing, Scoop?" Constable Bryant said.

"This isn't a game, sir," said John in his most grown-up voice.

"If this is a hoax, you kids are in big trouble."

We peered inside the small building. It was empty. The saboteur had fled.

CHAPTER 42 | John

"Thicker tree bark is said to indicate an early winter, but it may be that the trees are trying to grow a protective armor against shrapnel."—The Note Book, *Port Arthur Daily News*, 1915

"Saara, where's that piece of fabric?" I said. "Constable Bryant, we have proof."

She retrieved it, saying, "This is a pocket from the man's coat—we found it in that hedge over there."

"There are the ropes we used to tie his hands and feet," I said, pointing to the floor.

"What you are *alleged* to have done," said the eldest officer, shorter than Constable Bryant and the other man. "You children have quite the imaginations."

I remembered what *alleged* meant: possible, not for sure, NO PROOF. Then I said, "What about the photographs I took?"

The officers who didn't know me raised their eyebrows, not taking us seriously. Even Constable Bryant shook his head. Mama looked dazed and pulled me close to her.

"Mrs. Pekkonen took my camera to the Rexall store to

get the film developed," I said. "We'll have pictures of the saboteur later today."

"You're welcome to bring them by the police station," said the shortest policeman, "*should* they materialize."

"You've *got* to search for the man," Saara pleaded. "He threatened us."

Mr. Pekkonen added, "What if he threatens someone else? Or hurts someone?"

I could tell Constable Bryant was thinking hard. Their words must've struck a nerve. "All right," he said. "Everyone remain where you are. Men, comb the neighbourhood. See if you can find any trace of this phantom German."

Their search was over far too soon. The officers said they found no sign of the saboteur.

"How could a man with an injured foot leave no trail?" asked Saara. But they shrugged and left.

Later, Mrs. Pekkonen brought over my camera and the photographs. I tried paying for them, but she wouldn't take my money. I was so excited to see them, I tore the envelope. Then I groaned.

Saara craned her neck to see and said, "Oh, too bad."

The pictures of the saboteur were duds. So dark even we couldn't tell there was a man tied up on the ground. No proof.

"At least the one of me and Mikko turned out," said Saara. "And the ones of Sanni are clear."

Shaking my head, I said, "But they're not the ones we need right now." I thanked Mrs. Pekkonen for her trouble. She was making coffee and keeping Mama company.

I slouched on the sofa in the parlour. "What are we

going to do now, Saara? There's no way to convince the police."

"We both know the saboteur was here. It's up to us to find him. We're Papa's only hope." She grasped my hand and pulled me to my feet. "Let's go back to the shed and look for clues."

Back outside, we stared at the small building. Saara flinched when a squirrel scuttled across the roof. "Can you check inside?" she asked. "I just can't go in there after what he did."

"Okay." I slipped through the doorway but found nothing new.

"Where would he go?" Saara wondered out loud. "He's limping and his coat is dirty and tattered. In daylight someone might see him and get suspicious."

"So he'd look for somewhere to hide during the day and go farther after dark."

"Then we have no time to lose."

"Don't forget how hungry he was," I added.

"Right," said Saara, "and where would he get food? The gardens are almost bare."

"He'd look for a house with no one home and go in and eat their food—"

"Or he'd forget about food and hide in a vacant house—"

"There are lots with For Rent signs."

"That's clever, John. The closest one is Birgitta's old house."

We darted to the back fence. The house where Peter used to live looked sad and empty. There was no sign that anyone had come through there lately. We prob'ly guessed wrong.

But I climbed over the low fence anyway. Something in the overgrown grass caught my eye. I whispered, "There's something down there." I bent over and picked it up. It was a half-full Aspirin bottle. The paper label wasn't wrinkly and the print was all readable. That meant it wasn't lying there when it rained last night.

"He was here!" I exclaimed, starting off toward the house.

Saara grabbed the back of my shirt to stop me. She whispered loudly, "Whoa—we need a plan. If he's in the house, he'll likely move to another spot after dark. So we have to be smart and act fast and make sure he stays put until the police arrive."

"But the police won't come again—they'll think we're crying wolf."

"We'll worry about that later. First we have to know he's in there."

We crept toward the rear of the house. I nudged her arm, pointing to the back door. It had been forced open.

"We can't go inside," said Saara. "We can't risk him seeing us."

For a moment, it felt hopeless, like there was no way we could help Papa.

Then an idea came to me. "I know where we can see inside."

"We're not going to climb a tree, if that's what you're thinking."

"Nope, only stairs—in Fred's house!"

Saara glanced next door. I pointed to the second floor. There was a small window—a perfect lookout for spying. "Okay, let's go," she said.

We backtracked through Peter's yard. That's when we could see the flattened grass in the shadows next to the fence. No wonder the police hadn't seen his trail.

We hopped the fence and sped around to Fred's front door. My pal came when I knocked.

I blurted, "We need to spy on Peter's old house. We think the saboteur's in there."

Fred's eyes saucered. He whistled. "That sounds bully!" We followed him up the stairs.

The window was too high for us to see through. Fred fetched a wooden chair. Saara stood on the chair and said, "I can see part of the kitchen and ... part of an upstairs bedroom and ... oh."

"What do you see?" I asked.

"I'm spying on the bathroom!" she said, blushing.

"Good," said Fred. "Maybe he'll have to use it soon."

"But what about his privacy?" she said.

"Who cares?" I said. "He threatened you!"

"You try, John," she whispered, stepping off the chair.

I climbed up, rose on my tiptoes, and stared out the window.

"Can you see clearly?" she asked.

"Yup," I said. "Why are you whispering? He can't hear us."

"It helps me think better."

Me and Fred laughed.

After spying for ten minutes, I said, "My foot's getting

a cramp—we should have just looked in all the windows next door from the ground."

"What, and scare him off or get ourselves kidnapped again?" said Saara. "No, watching from here is better. I'll have a turn."

We switched places. Me and Fred sat on the floor.

How long would this take? We was sure the saboteur had been in the house. But was he still there? If he was, what if he slipped out one of the doors and stayed close to the house? He could escape without Saara seeing him.

"One of us should watch the front of the house from the ground, in case he tries to get away," I said.

Fred leaped to his feet. "I can do that," he said, running down the stairs.

"Saara, how're we going to get the police to come if we do see him in there?"

"Since they won't listen to us, we have to convince an adult to call them—someone they *will* believe."

"What about Mr. Pekkonen?" I said.

"No, they wouldn't come a second time for him," she said with a sigh. "The best person would be someone who's not an alien."

"You mean, like Principal Graham?"

"Yes, someone like him, but who's close by. We're running out of time."

Most of our neighbours was foreigners. Who else could we ask?

"Birgitta said they left cans of food there," said Saara. "I bet he's eating it." Then she turned to me and exclaimed, "Mr. Campbell! That's who could help us."

"Why him?"

"He bought the house this summer. The house has been broken into. He'll want the police to catch the person who damaged his property."

"Saara," I said, poking her leg, "you're supposed to be spying."

She whipped her head around and gasped. "There's someone in the bathroom."

"Let me see," I demanded. She helped me up to stand beside her. "Yup," I said, "and it's a man."

I jumped off the chair. "Saara, you go ask Mr. Campbell to call the police. Me and Fred will keep watch from outside, front and back. If he leaves, we'll follow him."

"Me? But Mr. Campbell won't talk to me—he ignores me. We haven't spoken since the day he told me his opinion of German-lovers."

"Look, I had to talk to Mr. McLeod, so it's your turn now."

"He's not going to listen to me," she said.

"Saara, quit wasting time arguing. Just go!"

CHAPTER 43 | Saara

"Swat the spies!"—The Note Book, *Port Arthur Daily News*, 1915

John was right—I had to try asking Mr. Campbell. I couldn't let Papa down. I raced outside, around the corner of our house, and halfway down the back lane before I slowed to think about what I would say. The sun was brushing the horizon.

At Mr. Campbell's back gate, I inhaled deeply, then stepped into his yard. I climbed his back steps and knocked on the door.

Mr. Campbell peeked out the kitchen window and scowled. "Go away. I don't want to talk to you."

"But it's important," I yelled. "It's about the house you own up the hill."

"What about it?" he asked gruffly, stepping outside.

"You need to call the police—a man broke in and he's still in there."

"How do you know?"

"I saw the damaged back door and saw the man through a window."

"What were you doing skulking around my rental property?"

I decided it would not be wise to tell him. "If you call the police right away, they might catch him."

"I'll catch the rotter myself!"

"No, Mr. Campbell. What if he's dangerous? You could get hurt. Just get the police."

He shook his head, saying, "First I want to see the damage."

"Then please go quickly," I cried.

He was no spring chicken, but he rushed as best he could up the hill to his property.

We found a gap in the hedge and peered at the back door. John was still posted in his lookout spot in Fred's backyard. That was a good sign—the saboteur hadn't left yet.

Mr. Campbell saw enough to convince him of the break-in. "How dare someone enter without permission. My neighbour has a telephone. I'll call the police from there."

He headed off, walking faster now.

I hunkered down in the grass with John to wait for the police. *Hurry, Mr. Campbell.*

This time we welcomed the patrol wagon on our side lane. Three police officers climbed out. I recognized the shortest one from earlier. He stayed at the front while the other two found the back door and entered the house.

Mr. Campbell joined the policeman out front. Gawking neighbours began arriving, including Mr. Pekkonen and a flushed and worried Mrs. Entwhistle. Then Mama appeared.

I held my breath, waiting for the officers to emerge. There were shouts … breaking glass.

"Get him!" said John.

The policemen barged out the back door. They were holding the man from the shed!

Mr. Campbell smiled when he saw them. "Good work, officers."

"Thank you for the tip, sir," said the shortest policeman. "We'll lock up this thief."

"He's more than a thief," shouted John, charging over.

I followed him and said, "He's the German who threatened us earlier. He sabotaged the grain elevator!"

Everyone turned to stare at us, including the "thief." He recognized us and spat something in German.

The short officer then zeroed in on the saboteur, demanding, "What is your name?"

No response.

"What were your whereabouts last evening between eight and nine o'clock?"

Silence.

The officer searched the man for identification but found none. What he did find tucked within an inside pocket of the man's torn black coat was all they needed. There were drawings of bridges and buildings, including several grain elevators, and directions on how to sabotage them. There was also a fuse.

"You are under arrest for sabotage against the Dominion of Canada."

John and Fred whooped. I hugged Mama. The officers loaded the suspect into the patrol wagon and drove away.

Fred playfully punched John on the arm, saying, "Now they'll let your father out of jail!"

Feeling a large hand on my shoulder, I spun around. It belonged to Mr. Campbell.

"Saara, I owe you an apology," he said. "And I'm grateful you alerted me to the break-in. Thank you."

"You're welcome. Thank you for believing me."

He cleared his throat and said, "I didn't know your father was arrested. May I drive you all to fetch him from the jail?"

"Yes, please!"

"Come with me." He turned to leave.

I quickly explained this to Mama in Finnish. Along the way to Mr. Campbell's residence, John and I filled her in on how we'd located the saboteur.

"*Kiitos. Kiitos paljon*," said Mama. "I'm so proud of you both."

The police did not release Papa right away. We had to wait outside for ages while they grilled the man we had helped them catch. And we weren't alone while we waited. A reporter from the *Daily News* was waiting, too. He kept glancing at John like he was going to say something, but he didn't.

Finally the door opened. There stood Papa. "The man they arrested today confessed," he said. "I'm free to go!"

Mama, John, and I swarmed him, all trying to hug him at once.

For a while Papa couldn't speak. Then the words

streamed out. "I feared I'd never leave this place, that I'd never see you again. Like that terrible time after the *Empress* sank when I didn't know whether any of you were still alive. Then the guard told me my own children caught the saboteur. How can that be true?"

John and I blurted bits of the story. It was chaos until Papa stopped us, saying, "Take turns and tell me everything."

When we were done, Papa hugged us both and said, "This calls for a celebration."

"Let's all go to see a moving picture," I said. "John's never seen one."

Papa said, "Tomorrow, that's what we'll do."

The grin on my brother's face looked like it would last all the way until then.

The next morning, birdsong stirred me from my sleep. I tried to slide back into my dream but couldn't. My brain was now too wide awake thinking about all that had happened since the Fall Fair.

Back when Miss Rodgers learned I was leaving school to help at the farm, she told me that sometimes my path must make a sharp twist to reveal my purpose. But what twists! First, the *Empress* shipwreck. Then Auntie's battle with tuberculosis. Now sabotage. After all of that, surely I could handle whatever school work Mr. Graham assigned. No twist in my path was going to stop me from reaching my goal: Miss Mäki, schoolteacher.

This time yesterday, my father had been locked in jail. Now Papa was free because of me and John. My brother had done a lot of growing up lately, pulling fewer pranks and being more useful. He reminded me of Canuck—small, but he had strength and pluck.

I stood and began dressing. My bedroom door flung open. *John!* Just in time, I snatched my quilt to cover up and yelled, "Hey—knock first!"

"Come quick—Sipu's hurt."

"Ha, ha. You already tried that prank on me. Go away."

"Saara, I'm not joking. She needs you."

"Why should I believe you this time?"

"Just come outside!" he said, sounding exasperated. He motioned with both arms to follow him, and then he flew down the steps.

I remembered Mikko's words: *A fellow wouldn't treat you that way if he didn't like you.* John only wanted a reaction. I decided to humour him. I finished dressing but refused to run.

There was no sign of my brother when I stepped out of the porch. I couldn't see him in the backyard, either. "John, where are you?" I called.

"Behind the shelter," he replied in a loud whisper.

When I reached him, he added, "Sipu's under there, moaning."

It was the strangest sound I'd ever heard her make. On my knees, I cooed to Sipu. She hissed. I should have gotten the hint, but instead I reached my hand toward her and she clawed me, hissing louder.

"Ouch! Okay, I'll leave you alone." I caught a glimpse of something shiny and wet. Sipu was licking it all over. "Come on, John. Sipu's just fine. We'll leave her in peace."

"She sounds hurt. We can't leave her," he said with genuine concern.

"She's not hurt—she's birthing her kittens."

"What? Are you pulling a prank on me?"

With a huge smile, I said, "No, I ain't."

He chuckled at my tease. "Good," he said, "'cause now you've got to read my front-page report on the saboteur. For once the *Daily News* got the facts exactly right."

The first Finnish immigrants to Canada arrived in the 1870s and settled in the Thunder Bay area in north-western Ontario. By 1913, about one out of every ten people living in Port Arthur (now part of Thunder Bay) was of Finnish origin. They chose the area for its employment opportunities and for the similarity of its landscape to their homeland. Finnish immigrants kept their language and culture alive. They were involved in their community, choosing from a variety of activities including Finnish church, the temperance movement, drama, music, sports, and labour organization. There is still a strong Finnish component to Thunder Bay. The Finnish Labour Temple, now called the Finlandia Club, hosts the Thunder Bay Finnish Canadian Historical Society museum, the Hoito Restaurant, and community social events in "the Big Finn Hall."

During the opening year of the First World War (1914–1915), massive layoffs of European immigrant workers occurred in major centres across Canada. A large number of men in Port Arthur lost their jobs. Many enlisted to fight in the war, while others left town in search of work. Food prices were rising and some goods were in short supply. War news dominated the headlines in the local newspapers.

In August 1914, the Canadian government invoked the War Measures Act. The newly appointed Canadian chief censor, Ernest J. Chambers, monitored newspapers and books to ensure nothing was printed that would hinder the war effort, and he banned publications that included objectionable material.

Rumours of German spies in Canada were rampant; it was feared they would sabotage key installations. Soldiers were posted to guard railways, bridges, canals, factories, power plants, wireless stations, and grain elevators. Port Arthur, along with its twin city, Fort William, was the major grain-handling centre in Canada, with large shipments to the Western Front to feed troops and animals.

Canadians grew increasingly nervous about and suspicious of the half million resident enemy aliens. Under the War Measures Act, enemy aliens were defined as natives of Germany and of the Austro-Hungarian Empire (the latter then simply referred to as Austrians). All were required to register at registration centres and report back monthly, carrying identity papers at all times. They were forbidden to leave Canada without permission. When a German torpedo sank the steamship *Lusitania* on May 7, 1915, large numbers of enemy aliens were dismissed from their jobs and then found it more and more difficult to obtain work. Businesses and ethnic facilities belonging to members of the German-Canadian community were damaged or destroyed.

Over the summer of 1915, suspicion of enemy aliens turned into widespread hysteria, with sabotage cited as the cause for every incident. For example, fires at important buildings such as grain elevators were blamed on saboteurs, when in fact the cause was human negligence, lightning, or a spark from the machinery igniting grain dust. While explosives were found planted on a number of ships destined for Europe, a discovery of suspicious liquids in glass bottles on one steamer proved to simply be liquid for refilling fire extinguishers on board.

In Canada and the United States, there was indeed a small network of saboteurs whose goal was to prevent troops and supplies from reaching Europe, or to delay them. These saboteurs made plans to attack Canadian railways, communication facilities, shipping locks, factories producing war supplies, and grain elevators. In August 1914, the Sault Ste. Marie and Port Arthur government wireless telegraph stations were attacked, and the saboteurs escaped. During the following month, a plot to dynamite the Welland Canal in Ontario was thwarted due to heightened security on site. On February 2, 1915, a saboteur named Werner Horn succeeded in bombing the Canadian Pacific Railway bridge linking St. Croix, New Brunswick, with Vanceboro, Maine, but the explosion had little effect. German agents Carl Schmidt and Gustav Stephen were arrested on March 19, 1915, for spying and plotting to blow up the Canadian Pacific Railway bridge in Nipigon, Ontario, 115 kilometres east of Port Arthur. Schmidt and Stephen later confessed to being part of the group that in June 1915 plotted against the Windsor Armouries in Windsor, Ontario, and dynamited a military uniform factory in Walkerville, Ontario.

Starting in 1914, certain enemy aliens were imprisoned in internment camps throughout Canada. At first, the individuals interned were those at risk to spy, commit sabotage, or leave Canada and fight on the enemy's side (primarily Germans), or those of any of the affected ethnic groups who were simply unemployed. But as suspicion mounted and the economy worsened, demand grew to intern more and more enemy aliens.

The majority of internees from the Thunder Bay area were sent to the internment camp at Kapuskasing, in northeastern Ontario. In May 1915, a number of Ukrainians in Fort William (now part of Thunder Bay) were so desperate for jobs, they petitioned the municipal government to intern them in order that they might work and they and their families be fed. For the German Kohse family in British Columbia, when Mr. Kohse was interned, his business, boat, and wealth were confiscated, and his wife and child did not receive financial support. Mrs. Kohse and her son had no choice but to join her husband at the Vernon Internment Camp, located in Vernon, British Columbia.

Eventually, across Canada, 8,579 men were interned, the majority of whom were of Ukrainian ethnicity, but also Germans, Austrians, Hungarians, Croatians, Serbs, Rumanians, Bulgarians, Jews, Poles, Turks, and others. Most were labourers with no anti-Canadian sentiments, imprisoned unjustly simply due to their nationality. Upon internment, the private property of these individuals was confiscated and some valuables were never returned. Most internees were required to do hard labour, and in the camps in the Rocky Mountains, internees reported being brutally treated and even tortured.

After the First World War ended, a small number of internees deemed dangerous or troublesome were deported, while 1,964 individuals (mostly Germans) were repatriated to Europe. Apart from the release dates of internees, the official internment records were destroyed by the Canadian government.

Of the twenty-four First World War internment camps in Canada, only two facilities housed women and children: those of Ukrainian ethnicity in the Spirit Lake Internment Camp, Spirit Lake, Quebec; and those of German ethnicity in the Vernon Internment Camp. A total of 81 women and 156 children were interned at these camps. The Vernon Internment Camp operated from September 18, 1914, until February 20, 1920. Its single male internees of non-German descent (primarily Ukrainians) were sent out to work camps. The Vernon Internment Camp remained open for two years following the end of the First World War in order to continue exploiting this forced labour for clearing land and building roads.

When civil war broke out in Finland early in 1918, because one faction sought military assistance from Germany, the government of Canada declared people of Finnish nationality living in Canada to be enemy aliens. All had their travel restricted, requiring a permit to leave Canada, and censorship of Finnish-language materials intensified.

The Girl Detective was a series of two-reel silent moving picture shows produced in the early 1900s. In these thrillers, the Girl Detective, a society girl, assists the police with solving crimes. For working-class people, live entertainment was often not affordable, whereas silent movies were within their means at five or ten cents for admission. For immigrants with limited English, this was an accessible form of entertainment which they could enjoy.

Further information can be found in the books and online resources listed below.

Spies and Sabotage

Secrets, Lies, Gizmos, and Spies: A History of Spies and Espionage by Janet Wyman Coleman

Spy, Spy Again: True Tales of Failed Espionage by Tina Holdcroft

Super Spies of World War I by Kate Walker and Elaine Argaet

Undated photo of soldiers guarding the grain elevators in the Thunder Bay area during the First World War (1914–1918): http://images.ourontario.ca/gateway/1708737/data?n=4 (click the image at right to enlarge)

Photo of a Canadian Pacific Railway train travelling over the Nipigon River railway bridge (1885): http://images.ourontario.ca/gateway/2303383/image/916945?n=13

Internment Camps

Prisoners in the Promised Land: The Ukrainian Internment Diary of Anya Soloniuk, Spirit Lake, Quebec, 1914 (Dear Canada Series) by Marsha Forchuk Skrypuch

List of internment camps in Canada during the First World War: http://www.internmentcanada.ca/resources-camp-list.cfm

Map of internment camps in Canada during the First World War: http://www.internmentcanada.ca/resources-map.cfm

Pamphlet with letter written by nine-year-old Katie Domytryk to her interned father: http://www.internmentcanada.ca/PDF/CFWWIRF_Pamphlet_English.pdf

Photo of the Vernon Internment Camp (1916) and undated group photo of a family of men, women, and children who were internees in the Vernon Internment Camp during the First World War (1914–1920): http://www.vernonmuseum.ca/ar_search.html (search with keyword: internment)

GLOSSARY OF FINNISH WORDS
AND PRONUNCIATION GUIDE

Note: As shown by the capital letters in the pronunciations, the emphasis is always on the first syllable in Finnish words. "K" in Finnish is a sound halfway between "k" and a hard "g"; in the guide below, it is represented by a "k" or a "c," depending on which makes the pronunciation clearer.

Joulupukki	YO-loo-poo-kee
	Santa Claus
kiitos	KEE-tohss
	thank you
kiitos paljon	KEE-tohss BALL-yone
	thank you very much
kulta	KOOL-tuh
	gold
Mitä ihmettä?	MI-ta IH-met-ta
	What on earth?
näkkileipä	NACK-ee-LAY-pa
	flat round rye bread, baked with a centre hole for threading onto a rod to dry, resulting in a thick crispbread
pulla	BOOL-uh
	sweet yeast bread flavoured with cardamom
voi	VOY
	oh!

ACKNOWLEDGEMENTS

My heartfelt thanks to my husband, Will, always the first and most enthusiastic audience of my writing—I cherish your feedback and support. To my daughter, Annaliis, and my son, Stefan, thank you for your ongoing interest in my writing projects and your encouragement.

I would like to thank the Okanagan Regional Library staff for research assistance; Ilkka Koskivuo for help with Finnish language questions; Helen and Jim Mulligan for introducing me to the Preventorium in Hamilton, Ontario; and Anita Lange for historical information about Nipigon. Thank you to Betty Brill, Curator, and Ai Oyakawa, Curatorial Assistant, Nipigon Historical Museum, for research and photographs of the Canadian Pacific Railway bridge at Nipigon, Ontario; Beverly Soloway, Elinor Barr, and Jean Morrison for help with researching the history of Thunder Bay; Tory Tronrud, Director/Curator, Thunder Bay Museum, for assistance with historical research and photographs. I am grateful to Ilene McKenna, Reference Archivist, Library and Archives Canada, and Marsha Skrypuch for information concerning the Vernon Internment Camp; Barbara Bell, Archivist, Greater Vernon Museum and Archives, and Andrea Malysh, Program Manager, Canadian First World War Internment Recognition

Fund, for research assistance and for reviewing the manuscript for accuracy regarding the Vernon Internment Camp; and Helmut Hesse, Tony Bergmeier, and Egon Stanik of the German-Canadian Congress for information regarding German-Canadian internees during the First World War. Thank you to Sharon Helberg for help with school questions; Sig Ottenbreit, volunteer at the Heritage classroom in Central School, Kelowna, B.C., for research assistance about school assignments; Marian Press, Acting Chief Librarian, and Kathy Imrie, Reference Services, Ontario Institute for Studies in Education Library, University of Toronto, for information regarding Ontario promotion examinations; and John Wilson for reviewing the manuscript for overall historical accuracy. Any errors that remain in the book are mine alone.

To April Kieke and Cameron Waller, thank you for asking me to give John a bigger role. I am sincerely grateful to Patricia Fraser, Eileen Holland, and Loraine Kemp for reviewing the manuscript and sharing valuable insights; to teacher-librarian Sarah Parmar and student editors Andrew Kates, Emma Parmar, and Emma Sieben for helpful feedback on the manuscript; and to Brynn Tucker for modelling as Saara. Mary Ann Thompson, your discerning eye throughout your generous and intensive critiques of the manuscript enabled me to strengthen the story—thank you.

Finally, thank you to Laura Peetoom for your inspired challenge to rewrite this book from Saara's *and* John's viewpoints—the story expanded in surprising ways; Dawn Loewen for your in-depth and meticulous copyedit; Frances Hunter for your top-quality layout work and book design; and my publisher, Diane Morriss, for your warm encouragement, support, and enthusiasm during the creation of this book. I am privileged to work with all of you.

Canadian Pacific Railway bridge over Nipigon River, Ontario (1910). This bridge required two years to construct.
— COURTESY NIPIGON HISTORICAL MUSEUM ARCHIVES, DH4

Canadian Pacific Railway bridge over Nipigon River, Ontario (1936).— COURTESY NIPIGON HISTORICAL MUSEUM ARCHIVES, NMP 1255

Port Arthur government wireless station, Port Arthur, Ontario (1913).
— COURTESY THUNDER BAY HISTORICAL MUSEUM SOCIETY, 979.1.29

Canadian Northern Railway grain elevator at the foot of Bay Street (also known at various times as the Canadian Government elevator and Saskatchewan Pool 6), Port Arthur, Ontario (1914).— COURTESY THUNDER BAY HISTORICAL MUSEUM SOCIETY, 974.55.57

Current River swimming pool, Port Arthur, Ontario (August 2, 1926).— COURTESY THUNDER BAY HISTORICAL MUSEUM SOCIETY, 978.1.182

Photo postcard showing the houses, gardens, and main holding area of the Vernon Internment Camp, Vernon, B.C. (1916).—COURTESY VERNON MUSEUM AND ARCHIVES, PHOTO NO. 2500

Vernon Internment Camp escapees caught at Lois (Carmi), B.C. (1916). The prisoners had escaped by digging a tunnel with a homemade wooden auger. A breadbox in the kitchen disguised the entrance to the tunnel.—COURTESY VERNON MUSEUM AND ARCHIVES, PHOTO NO. 21935

Candid photo of a family at the Vernon Internment Camp standing in front of the canvas-roofed houses, Vernon, B.C. (circa 1917).—COURTESY VERNON MUSEUM AND ARCHIVES, PHOTO NO. 11969

Fred Kohse and Victor Heiny, internees at the
Vernon Internment Camp, Vernon, B.C. (circa
1916).—COURTESY THE PRIVATE COLLECTION OF
ANDREA MALYSH

The author next to the Vernon Internment Camp plaque located on the grounds of W. L. Seaton High School and MacDonald Park, Vernon, B.C. The commemorative marker reads: "VERNON INTERNMENT CAMP Thousands of Ukrainian Canadians and other European immigrants were unjustly imprisoned as 'enemy aliens' during Canada's first national internment operations of 1914-1920. This plaque is dedicated to the memory of the men, women and children who were held at the Vernon internment camp, on this location, now known as MacDonald Park, between 18 September 1914 and 20 February 1920. Placed by the Vernon Branch of the Ukrainian Canadian Congress in cooperation with the Ukrainian Canadian Civil Liberties Association and the Ukrainian Canadian community of British Columbia. 7 June 1997."—WILL AUTIO PHOTO

Permit to leave Canada on or before the 2nd day of July

..., is hereby granted to Jack Keto 1st July 1918.

(In corresponding about this permit refer to both name and serial number.)

6658

PERMIT TO LEAVE CANADA

(Schedule B. to Order in Council P. C. 1433 of May 24, 1917.)

"Any person to whom such written permission to leave Canada has been granted shall carefully preserve the same and keep it always about his person.—(Sec. 3, Sec. Order-in-Council 1433.)"

I, Jack Keto of Nipigonyia, Port Arthur, (if town or city give street address). in the Province of Ontario, make oath and do say that I was born at Finland on the 27th day of July 18 86, that I am a (an) Canadian (subject) (citizen) by (birth) (naturalization); that I have resided at the above address for 14 years, that I am personally known to and refer for identification to :—

Wm McKirdy, of Nipigon, Ontario
John Barry, of Port Arthur, Ontario
G. L. Bliss of Nipigon, Ontario
John G. McKirdy, of Nipigon, Ontario

that I desire permission to leave Canada to go to Duluth, Minn., U.S. (Give address in full) for the purpose of Visiting friends that I wish to be absent from Canada for two weeks (Length of absence)

My height is 5' 6"; my weight is 140
My eyes are blue; my hair is fair
My occupation is Farmer
I am (married) (single) (widower) (widow)
I have one children living.

The attached photograph is a good likeness of me taken 18 (months) (days) ago.

And I make this solemn declaration conscientiously believing it to be true and correct and knowing that it is of the same force and effect as if made under oath and by virtue of the Canada Evidence Act.

Declared before me at Port Arthur, in the Province of Ontario this ... day of July 19...

J. Keto
Signature of Applicant.

D. F. Warren
Immigration Agent.

I have been personally acquainted with the above-mentioned applicant for a period of (years) (months). I recognize the above attached photo as a true likeness of him. I believe the statements which he makes above to be correct and have seen him in my presence attach his signature on the same line on which my own appears.

J. Keto
Signature of Applicant.

D. F. Warren
Signature of Immigration Agent, Chief of Police, Clergyman or Dominion Government Officer.

"Permit to Leave Canada" for an enemy alien born in Finland, issued to Jack Keto (foster father to the author's paternal grandmother) on July 1, 1918.
—COURTESY ANITA LANGE

Karen Autio holding a reproduction of the *Port Arthur Daily News* from March 19, 1915, with the headline "*SPIES, EQUIPPED FOR BRIDGE WRECKING, ARRESTED IN PORT ARTHUR.*"
—WILL AUTIO PHOTO

Karen Autio grew up in Nipigon, Ontario. She had heard of the planned sabotage attempt on the Canadian Pacific's Nipigon River railway bridge during the First World War, but she had difficulty believing it truly happened. While researching her previous book, Karen found confirmation of the 1915 event. German agents were arrested and confessed to spying and conspiring to destroy the railway bridge so they could prevent the movement of soldiers eastward. Discovering this information led Karen to additional research which inspired this book.

Sabotage is the third book in the trilogy that tells the Mäki family's story. The first two books are *Second Watch* (Sono Nis Press, 2005) and *Saara's Passage* (Sono Nis Press, 2008), both shortlisted for the Chocolate Lily Award.

Karen lives in Kelowna, British Columbia. To learn more about Karen Autio and her books, visit www.karenautio.com.